In a blue velvet dress

In a Blue Velvet Dress

Catherine Sefton

HYPERION

NEW YORK

Text © 1972, 1973 by Catherine Sefton
First published by Harper and Row, Publishers, Inc. © 1972, 1973. Reprinted by permission of HarperCollins Publishers, Inc.

First Volo edition 2002
1 3 5 7 9 10 8 6 4 2

Printed in the United States of America
The text for this book is set in 13-point Deepdene.

ISBN 0-7868-1693-7
Library of Congress Catalog Card Data on file.

Visit www.volobooks.com

For Fionnuala
to whom it could have happened

Know that my sweet Mary
is the owner of this book.
If anyone should steal it
'twas from Mary it was took.

CHAPTER ONE

ANE REID WAS eleven years old. She was short, she was thin, and she always had her head in a book. She often fell over things because she wouldn't look where she was going.

"Not that there's much to look at here," she said glumly, staring out through the car window at the main street of Rathard. If she hadn't been sitting in the car she would probably have fallen over something there and then, for her head went straight back into her book. She was still reading when the car pulled to a stop outside 3 Mole Street.

"Out you get, Jane," said Albert Hildreth.

Out she got, with her head immersed in her book.

"Have you got your things?" said Albert.

"Hmmh?" said Jane.

Albert took the book from her and closed it, firmly. "Your things, Jane," he said. "Are you *sure* you've got them?"

She had not.

"Your precious books!" exclaimed Albert, who never had time to read anything because he was kept so busy being Albert. He was Head Fireman, Coxswain of the Lifeboat, and Chief Odd Jobs Man to the town of Rathard. He enjoyed hammering things, and working with engines. He wasn't at all like Jane's father, who thought that spanners were for eating Spanish food with.

Jane got her things out of the car. She had one *small* suitcase full of clothes and one *large* suitcase full of books, which was so heavy that Albert Hildreth had to carry it for her. Mr. and Mrs. Reid had gone to Scotland in Uncle Tom's boat, and the Hildreths had agreed to look after Jane until they came back, which didn't please Jane one bit. Crossing the Irish Sea on

The Seagull would have been fun, while staying in Rathard, she was convinced, wouldn't be. For a start the only book in the entire house was the Telephone Directory, which Jane had read twice over on her last visit to Mole Street. So, on the day her parents were to leave for Scotland, Jane took out her biggest suitcase and made a careful tour of the house, picking out the books she liked best.

"But you'll only be there a few days, and there's the sea and tennis and . . . and country walks!" said her mother, following her around in despair.

"I don't like looking at cows," said Jane. She had half a notion that cows might bite her given the chance, and she preferred sitting at home with a good book to risking it. Only twenty-nine of her hundred and thirty-one books would fit into the suitcase but she hoped that, by reading through the better ones two or three times, she would somehow manage to live through her stay at 3 Mole Street.

Off went the Reids to Scotland on *The Seagull* and off went Jane to Rathard—reluctantly.

She was not interested in the lighthouse or the harbor, or the castle on its hill behind the town. She was not interested in the farmhouses or the fields she passed on the way to Rathard; she had no desire to fish or climb mountains. She ate her dinner in silence, thanked Mrs. Hildreth very politely, helped with the washing up, and disappeared up the narrow staircase of the old house to her own room.

"Well, I never," said Mrs. Hildreth, clucking her tongue between her teeth.

"I'm sure I don't know, Maisie," said Albert, who had just taken the grandfather clock to pieces and lost a vital bit under the sofa. He took a long time to find it and smeared oil all over the hearth rug and the cat, but he enjoyed himself, getting crosser and crosser.

Mrs. Hildreth wondered if she ought to go upstairs and speak to the child, but she decided that she would not.

A good thing too!

Jane Reid, bookworm, might have been exceedingly rude to her.

Jane Reid, bookworm, was standing over an open suitcase, speechless in the face of disaster.

The suitcase contained five shirts, two pairs of trousers neatly folded, and a cardboard box full of her father's rock samples.

Meanwhile, on board *The Seagull*, Mr. Reid was staring aghast at a suitcase full of *Chalet School* Stories, Pamela Brown books, and lots of others.

"Where are my rocks?" he cried to his wife.

"Where are my books?" Jane would have cried, if there had been anyone to cry it to, but there wasn't.

No books! It was nothing less than a tragedy, a disaster!

There was only one thing for it. She would have to scour Rathard in search of a bookshop. She had fifty pence exactly to last her until her parents came back, and now it would all have to go on books.

Three Mole Street had walls that were four feet thick, and that meant that the windows had wide sills on the inside, the sort you can sit on. Jane climbed up on the sill in her room and looked out at the High Street. Boot shops, sweet shops, fruit shops, butcher shops, but not a single solitary bookshop.

She clambered down from the sill and went over to her other suitcase, which she unpacked, putting the things carefully away in the chest of drawers which Mrs. Hildreth had left empty for her. It was painted white and looked very shiny and pretty with a dainty lace runner laid on top. The room was a gleaming buttercup yellow, with pale curtains and a fleecy white eiderdown on the little bed.

"Nice for the child," thought Mrs. Hildreth, though Mrs. Reid could have told her a thing or two about Jane and white paint.

It was a nice room, a sunny room, with all

the hustle and bustle of a little seaside town going on outside the windows. It looked out on the High Street and, over the roofs of the houses, at the harbor with its white lighthouse, very much like a saltcellar. She could see people walking about doing their shopping, and trucks unloading by the pier, and there was an old lady in a yellow suit who drove her car as though she *wanted* to run everyone over.

It was a nice town, but Jane Reid didn't see it that way.

A town with no library.

A town with no bookshop.

She went downstairs again, feeling the old boards creak under her feet. Jane lived in a modern bungalow and she thought that people who lived in houses with stairs were a bit peculiar. Stairs take such a lot of getting up.

Albert Hildreth had somehow got his head stuck inside the case of the grandfather clock and all he said when she asked him about bookshops in Rathard was "Ha!" which wasn't very helpful to a dismayed bookworm.

"Going for a walk, dear?" said Mrs. Hildreth, peering round the door of the kitchen. "Don't interrupt your Uncle Albert now, he's busy."

Jane went into the kitchen to talk to her. It was a long low room with huge rafters supporting the roof and a big black stove in one corner, not at all like the kitchen at home. But then nothing in 3 Mole Street was like home. It was an old house with walls thick enough for secret staircases, with stone floors, and crooked windows and doors. It was the sort of house that had probably been there almost forever. It was the sort of house where busy people said "Ha!" and went on with what they were doing, instead of being helpful.

There wasn't really anything wrong with the house at all, but Jane didn't want to own up to being homesick.

"Are there any bookshops in Rathard?" Jane said.

"Not that I know of, dear," said Mrs. Hildreth. "We're too busy here to bother with such things."

"I suppose you have *a* book," Jane said nastily, because she was still annoyed about picking up her father's suitcase instead of her own and about being in a strange house and homesick and a bit lonely. It was a very old joke, but Mrs. Hildreth didn't seem to know it.

"We used to have one," she said, quite seriously. "Someone borrowed it. One of the Smollets, I suppose."

"I suppose there might be a bookshop hidden away somewhere, one you haven't noticed?"

"There *might* be," Mrs. Hildreth said.

So Jane went off to search for it, just in case.

All along the High Street, as far as the castle gates. Then down by Castle Street and Manor Street to the sea front and back past Gurney's Amusements through Union Street to the Hildreths'.

Not a bookshop in sight.

There was a newspaper shop with some paperback books, the least expensive of which was *Viennese Cooking* and cost thirty-eight pence.

"It looks a bit dog-eared to me," said Jane, hoping to strike a bargain, but the shopman would have none of it.

"Looked quite upset, she did," he told his wife, when Jane left the shop.

She would have paid thirty-eight pence for it, but she loathed cooking, which interfered with good reading time.

In disgust, Jane went down to the harbor and read the names on all the boats, including Albert's lifeboat, *Sir Henry King*, which looked very smart and efficient in blue and red and gray. She spent half an hour in Gurney's Amusements and lost one penny, which was one more than she felt she could afford. She wandered down onto the beach to look for crabs, but she couldn't find any. She looked at the souvenir shops, and bought a postcard showing the town and the mountains to send to her mother.

Then she went back to 3 Mole Street.

"Did you have a nice walk, dear?" said Mrs. Hildreth anxiously. She spent most of her life worrying about people, even when there was nothing to worry about.

Jane was about to say "no" when Albert gave a great howl, and came hopping into the kitchen on one foot, the one he hadn't dropped the weight of the grandfather clock onto.

Jane ate her tea in silence, and spent the next three hours reading the *Radio Times* four times from cover to cover. The television set had been broken for at least three months since Albert tripped over it when he was rearranging the furniture, but Mrs. Hildreth still went on buying the *Radio Times* out of habit.

"I think I'll just go to bed now, if I may, Mrs. Hildreth," Jane said, and she trotted off upstairs.

"Poor child," said Mrs. Hildreth, who was

very fond of children and longed . . . oh how she longed . . . for one of her own. "I'm afraid that Jane is bored with no one to play with."

"She reads, she doesn't play," said Albert. "'Tisnt natural, if you ask me."

At that moment Jane was sitting up in bed reading the cleaner's tab on the sheets. She'd already tried the Telephone Directory, but she really couldn't stick that. She'd also written her postcard.

> Daddy and Mummy,
>
> Having a lovely time here. Wish you were back. If you're going to be away a long time can you please please post back some of my books?
>
> Love XOXOXOXO Jane

She wasn't having a lovely time.

She did wish they were back. She wished it very much indeed.

No books.

She lay back on the little white bed and gazed at the ceiling. This holiday was going to be absolutely awful. She almost wished that it were time to go back to school. Then she thought about it, and didn't. She switched off the bedside lamp, and closed her eyes, determined to get off to sleep somehow.

Perhaps she did go to sleep; she could never be quite sure about it afterwards.

What she was sure about was that something disturbed her. She opened her eyes and lay there in the darkness. Then she reached out and switched on the lamp.

And she saw a book. It lay on the bedside table, close to her hand. It was a very small book, in a faded brown cover. She opened it eagerly, and read the title:

THE BRACELETS
or
HABITS OF GENTLENESS
by
Miss Edgeworth

She read it, all of it, in ten minutes.

It was a very short book.

It was also a very boring book.

But it *was* a book.

She slipped it beneath her pillow and went to sleep.

In the morning, when she went to look for it, the book was gone.

CHAPTER TWO

HERE HAD THE book come from? Where did it disappear to? It was a book, the only book she was likely to get, and Jane naturally wanted to know the answers to these questions. She meant to ask Mrs. Hildreth about it at breakfast, but something else happened which put it right out of her mind.

"This is William Smollet, Jane," said Mrs. Hildreth. "He's come to play."

Jane looked at William Smollet and William Smollet looked at Jane.

She saw a horrible little monster with a red bow tie and a gleaming white summer shirt and shorts. Mrs. Smollet had done her best with

William. He looked disgustingly clean and orderly, and very much as if *he* didn't think much of *her*.

He saw a broomstick with fat braids and big ears who looked too old to be sensible. Girlish and bossy, he thought, and the expression on her face told him plainly that *she* didn't like the look of *him* either.

"William is ten," said Mrs. Hildreth, hopefully.

"And a half," said William.

"I'm eleven," said Jane. "Pleased to meet you, I'm sure." She held out her hand.

"Delighted," said William, shaking it limply.

They both thought "liar" but they didn't say it. They were both being polite, well brought up, and well behaved—and weighing up the chances. Jane was older and had more experience, but William was nippy on his feet and took boxing lessons. He thought that he could handle her, despite the age and height advantage.

"I'm sure you'd love to take Jane for a walk, wouldn't you, William?" said Mrs. Hildreth. "William knows all the interesting places," she added hopefully, but Jane didn't seem to be excited by the idea.

"That would be lovely," she said, though she thought it would be anything but.

William said nothing. Nick, Addie, Sid, and Bopper were playing football at that very moment in Steward's field, and later on they planned an expedition to the ruins of Rathard House. He was dressed in his pinky-whites, looking as though butter wouldn't melt in his mouth, and determined to do something so nasty to Jane that he would never again be subjected to the indignity of entertaining one of Mrs. Hildreth's many child visitors. People had a habit of sending their children to stay with Mrs. Hildreth, because she liked having children around the house. If a brother got sick, or people had to go away, it was off to Mrs. Hildreth's with the family. Mrs. Hildreth's visitors were a terrible nuisance to the local children, and the Smollet family in particular. There were eight Smollets, and they were forever being sent down to 3 Mole Street to entertain waifs and strays.

As far as William was concerned, Jane Reid could go and jump off the pier. He wanted to go on the expedition to the ruins of Rathard House.

"Do you play football?" he said, not very hopefully, as they walked down toward the sea front.

Jane said nothing. He was too small to be seen talking to.

She had better things to do.

She might . . . well, she might. . . .

She might find something to read somewhere, if she was lucky. Anything would be better than walking babies round the town, and doing up their shoelaces for them.

"Can you do up your shoelaces?" said Jane, who had a cousin named Davenport who couldn't.

"Of course," said William. "I'll do yours up for you if you can't," he added helpfully.

"Don't be cheeky," said Jane.

This time William said nothing. He considered himself one up, which was a nice position to be in.

Jane pursed her lips and waited. She was one down, but she wasn't going to be one down for long. A lot of her annoyance at being stuck in Rathard suddenly came to the boil, and poor William just happened to be in the way at the time.

She waited until they were walking past a particularly smelly patch of seaweed and tar on the beach, where she slipped, banged into William, and bowled him over.

Tar on his white trousers, tar on his shirt, tar in his hair, and seaweed in his mouth. It was *unfortunate* that Jane had slipped, and even more *unfortunate* that she sat down on William Smollet afterwards.

"I'm *so* sorry, William," she said.

William got up and took the seaweed out of his mouth, but there wasn't much he could do about the tar.

"It is all my fault," said Jane happily, helping to brush William down by giving him heavy bangs on the back.

"Never mind," said William, sounding exactly like Mrs. Hildreth being polite, "think nothing of it."

He thought quite a lot of it.

He did not exactly trip Jane, or so he maintained, but somehow she landed upside down in the middle of a large wave, when all she had meant to do was paddle.

"Oh dear," he said innocently, "did you slip?"

Jane got to her feet. She was soaked to the skin. She had swallowed a lot of salt water. She had been tripped.

"You did that on purpose!" she snapped.

"You pushed me in the tar!" said William, equally cross.

"Serves you right," said Jane.

"Yah!" said William.

"Yah yourself!" said Jane, who was too excited to think of anything sharper to say, though she could have done much better given time to think about it.

"I take boxing lessons," said William, squaring up to her and bouncing forward.

It was unfortunate that he bounced forward onto a jellyfish, for he had to bounce back very quickly again, and in the process he got his feet tangled up and fell over in the shallow water.

"That will teach you not to hit a girl," said Jane, who hadn't been hit, thanks to the mushy intervention of the jellyfish, but felt that being almost hit was much the same thing anyway.

William got to his feet.

He was dripping wet, tar-stained, and one down, definitely.

Jane was only dripping wet, although there was slightly more of her to be dripping wet.

It wasn't fair.

But Jane looked very cross, and boxing lessons or no boxing lessons he had a feeling that he might come off the worse if they had a fight, or else she might cry.

"I hate you," he said, keeping his distance.

"And I hate you," panted Jane.

"I'm going," said William grandly.

"Then go!" said Jane.

William walked away. Then he stopped and looked back.

"You won't go telling, will you?" he said.

Jane shook her head nobly.

"I will tell them that I had an accident," said William with dignity. He was always having accidents of one sort or another anyway, and the Smollet authorities were used to it.

"I will too," said Jane.

"You'll die if you don't change out of those wet clothes," said William, hopefully.

"I am a very healthy person, thank you," said Jane. "I certainly don't need the advice of exceedingly silly little boys."

William stuck his tongue out at Jane, and Jane threw half a nearby sand castle at William.

Home, dripping wet, to face the music.

Mrs. Hildreth wasn't pleased. She gave Jane a brisk toweling and set her down before the fire with a hot orange drink while she argued with Albert about whether she *ought* to call the doctor, in case the poor child had caught a chill.

Mrs. Smollet, who had seven other Smollets to take care of in addition to William, dealt with the matter in a much more practical way. It was unpleasant and doesn't bear description, but William had lived through worse and came out not at all cowed. He went to bang the punching bag (a pillow hanging from the apple tree on a length of rope) in the backyard by the hay shed and took it out on Jane in a right and proper manner, befitting a future heavyweight champion of Ireland.

It wasn't William's fault that the pillow burst.

He didn't mean to fill the yard with feathers.

But Mrs. Smollet dealt with him for the second time in twenty minutes, in a practical way.

Meanwhile Jane Reid, the cause of all his trouble, was sitting on the roof of 3 Mole Street, helping Albert Hildreth to mend the hole through which part of the chimney had fallen. It was a very old house, the sort of house where things like the chimney falling into the attic happen now and then. The Hildreths hadn't much money and they had to put up with it; but even if they had had a lot of money, they would not have left the old house in Mole Street. They were much too fond of it to consider moving into a newfangled bungalow like the Reids', with no stairs.

From her perch on the roof Jane could see Scotland, where her mother and father were. It was no more than a distant gray shape on the horizon, but here and there she could make out a white speck which might or might not be a

house. She thought about her parents, and that
led her to think about her books, and *The
Bracelets* by Miss Edgeworth.

"What sort of a book?" said Albert, only
half listening. He didn't feel absolutely obliged
to take in every word, especially when she got
onto the subject of books—which was a subject
she very seldom got *off*. She was without doubt
the bookiest child he had ever met, taking after
her father and mother. The Hildreths liked the
Reids, but thought them very peculiar. It was
not a bad arrangement all round, for the Reids
liked the Hildreths but thought them, well . . .
odd.

"They read," said the Hildreths, "just like
their name."

"They don't read," said the Reids. "Can't
think how they put the day in."

"It was a Victorian children's book," said
Jane.

"Where did you get it?"

"Here," said Jane, but Albert didn't hear

what she said, for at that moment his foot went through the slates with half his body after it, leaving him half in and half out of the attic, with his feet kicking wildly round the light bulb and his two arms hugging what was left of the chimney stack.

Even Jane could see that it was no time to talk about books.

That night, before going to bed, Jane made a careful inspection of her bed, to find out if the book had somehow slipped down inside it.

No book.

It was most disappointing.

She could only imagine that the Hildreths must have meant the book as a once-only surprise, or perhaps they had borrowed it from a neighbor who wanted it back—though the book was so boring that only a book-mad neighbor would have wanted it back, and Rathard didn't strike Jane as the sort of place that is full of book-mad neighbors.

Half an hour later, when Jane had almost dozed off, she thought she heard something stir in the room.

"Who's that?" she said.

No one answered.

It was a bit frightening, and she groped out for the light and switched it on, expecting burglars or worse.

No one was there, except herself.

The book, which lay on her bedside table, was called:

THE DARLINGS OF THE NATIONS
by
Dora Nesbitt Kemp

Like *The Bracelets* it was old, and a bit boring, but better than nothing. It was about Nelson, Napoleon, Washington, and Peter the Great, and she read it from cover to cover.

Then she went to sleep.

In the morning, it was gone.

CHAPTER THREE

HAT, DEAR?" SAID Mrs. Hildreth, when Jane asked her about the books.

"*The Darlings of the Nations* and *The Bracelets*," Jane said. "Have you seen them around the house anywhere?"

"But I thought you'd forgotten your books, dear," said Mrs. Hildreth. "Didn't you grumble about mixing up your suitcases?"

Jane suspected that Mrs. Hildreth might have got hold of some books without telling Albert about them, knowing the way he felt about children who read when they could be doing something useful like mending roofs. "Wasting money!" he might have called it. It was possible that Mrs. Hildreth was slipping the books into her room at night and spiriting them away before morning so that Albert wouldn't see them.

It was possible, but not at all probable.

The Hildreths simply didn't work that way. They didn't say much, but they were still very fond of each other and got on well in their old house. Hiding things from each other wasn't like them at all.

But.

But.

Somebody had to be responsible for the disappearing books, and if it wasn't the Hildreths, who on earth was it?

"I wondered if perhaps there might be some old books lying in the attic you'd forgotten about," Jane said tentatively, giving Mrs. Hildreth a last chance to own up.

"Oh no, dear," said Mrs. Hildreth. She was worried about her guest, who should have been getting good fresh air, instead of mooning around the house looking for old books.

After lunch, Jane went wandering out of the house and up toward the castle, almost getting run over by the old lady in the yellow suit who was whizzing around town in her sports car again. The castle was well kept, and quite safe, so that she knew there was no danger in scrambling up the winding stone staircase inside the walls. But it felt as if it were dangerous. From the battlements she could see more of Scotland than was visible from the roof of 3 Mole Street, and out in the bay she could see Hammer Island with its lighthouse standing guard over a fringe of dangerous-looking rocks, and the bobbing buoys that marked the deep channel into Belfast Lough. Standing up there she might have been a Norman lady keeping watch for fierce Scots raiders coming to burn Rathard and take away all the people to be slaves. She would rush down into the banqueting hall and call out all her knights to beat off the raiders, and all the people of Rathard would be saved except William Smollet.

It was a satisfactory notion and she enjoyed it, although she came to a private decision that nothing too awful would happen to William Smollet. Nothing worse than, say, having his ears cut off. He might even manage to get himself rescued, after the raiders had knocked him about a bit.

Then she found something to read. It was a bronze plaque mounted on the wall of the Abbot's tower, and it said:

RATHARD CASTLE

This Castle was built in the early 13th C. by Sir Robert de Quinton, a Norman knight who was granted the town and barony of Rathard by King John. Later it was partially destroyed and fell into disuse. It was presented to the people of Rathard by the Quinton family and is now administered by the Commissioner for Ancient Monuments, who was responsible for its restoration.

Commission for Ancient Monuments

1936

How nice it would have been, Jane thought, to be a de Quinton, and live in a castle.

But the Reids were not Normans.

Scots.

So, far from being a Norman lady keeping watch, she would have been a fierce Scots raider cutting William Smollet's ears off and knocking him about a bit.

She was thinking about this as she walked back to the stair turret. Then she just happened to glance in the direction of 3 Mole Street.

A little girl was standing at the window of her room, a little girl with dark hair and a blue dress, looking out of the window at the sea.

"Cheek!" Jane thought, wondering who she could be. "Another Smollet, I suppose. Typical!" She made up her mind there and then to stay out for a good bit longer and avoid this latest example of the fighting Smollet family. It was five o'clock when she got back to Mole Street, and there wasn't hide nor hair of a Smollet to be seen.

Mrs. Hildreth must have been annoyed, but she certainly didn't give any indication of it, and she didn't mention the girl who had been prying in Jane's room.

Neither did Jane.

It was not a satisfactory day for Jane. She wanted to come out with a straight question about the two books, but she didn't think it would be a wise thing to do, if Mrs. Hildreth was trying to keep the books a secret from Albert. She thought she might try searching the old house high and low, but she couldn't do that without a very good reason. It wasn't her house, and the books weren't her books. She had no right to them at all.

Then the thought struck her, "If there are two books in the house, there might be more."

Perhaps there would even be one that *wasn't* boring.

"Like what?" she thought to herself.

She set off on one of her favorite games: Books I Like. There was *The Hobbit*, of course, and *The Lord of the Rings*. *Anne of Green Gables*. All the *Chalet School* Stories. Some Enid Blyton. *The Lion, The Witch and the Wardrobe*. *The Family at One End Street*. Books about real people. *Winnie-the-Pooh* (although she was supposed to be too old for it). *David Copperfield* (although she was supposed to be too young). *The Rider on the White Horse*. *The Brumby*. *The Story of the Amulet*. *The Gray Goose of Kilnevin*. Nearly all Meta Mayne Reid and not *Alice in Wonderland*.

And lots more.

She decided that if she had to choose one and only one of them, it would be *The Story of the Amulet* by E. Nesbit. The characters were interesting, and the book was just about the right length, and the Psammead was in it.

Jane was just about to tell Mrs. Hildreth the stories of all the Psammead books when Albert came bouncing down the stairs, looking for his hammer. At once the entire household was up in arms, rushing around here and there to find it, while Albert fumed and scolded. Jane helped with the search, but she kept her eyes open for books all the time, just in case. She didn't find the hammer because Albert had absentmindedly dropped it into the whitewash bucket when he was fixing a piano in the yard—it never did play properly again, but it looked as if it might.

Jane didn't find the books either.

That night she went to bed early.

There were no books underneath the pillow, or in the blankets, or in any of the drawers, or under the bed, or under the carpet, or behind the curtains, or in her suitcase, or beneath the broken floorboard, or hidden up the chimney, or wrapped in her pajamas.

She knew, because she looked and looked.

Then she got into bed, but she didn't switch off the light. She was determined to catch the book bringer book-handed.

Later, much later, there was a gentle knock on the door.

"At last," Jane thought, expecting that Mrs.

Hildreth was about to explain everything, and hand over the precious volume for the night.

"Can't you sleep, dear?" said Mrs. Hildreth. "Shall I fetch you a nice warm drink?"

"I'm quite all right, thank you, Mrs. Hildreth," said Jane, more than ever convinced that she knew where the books came from.

"Are you quite sure?" said Mrs. Hildreth. It would never do if anything happened to the child while her parents were away.

"Yes," said Jane, craftily pretending to be much sleepier than she was.

Mrs. Hildreth switched off the light and went back downstairs.

"*Now,*" Jane thought. She lay on, determined to stay awake, but gradually getting sleepier and sleepier. The old house was full of comfortable creaking noises and she felt very much a part of it as she lay in the white bed, as though she were surrounded by friends. It was, Jane thought, positively the friendliest-*feeling* house she could remember, maybe because it was so old. It wasn't so much the Hildreths—although the Hildreths were nice—but the spirit of the house itself. Old stone walls to keep out the cold, thick doors, and narrow stairways. Nice . . . yet so unlike her own home. She was missing her own home very much, despite all the niceness of 3 Mole Street.

Then. . . .

"Who's that?" Jane said, surprised out of her doze by something, she couldn't quite tell what. It was a rustle in the room, no more— like the swish of a long dress.

She switched on the light.

There was, of course, no one there.

How could there be? The door was closed, and Jane was sure that she would have heard it open. But there was something strange about the room, a certain fragrance, a scent of . . . of what?

She didn't know. It was familiar, but she couldn't for the life of her think what it was.

Then she saw the book.

It had been laid out on the washstand where she was sure to see it.

THE PHOENIX AND THE CARPET
by
E. Nesbit

Jane was pleased, although she'd read it once before. The Psammead books are easily readable several times, especially when you've forgotten bits of them.

She fetched it from the washstand, which had a large porcelain basin and a jug that was filled every morning with steaming warm water so that she could wash in her room. This was because the Hildreths' house was so old that it had no bathroom. All their water came from a tap in the yard, and had to be heated up with kettles. Jane thought that this arrangement was very odd, but the Hildreths didn't seem to mind. One thing about it though . . . it did suggest a way that the book might have come into the room. Suppose Mrs. Hildreth had hidden it inside the big water basin, and slipped it out when she came in to speak to Jane?

It was possible.

Only just.

Books don't move about on their own. They can be thrown, pushed, carried, or conceivably dropped on top of people, but there has to be someone doing the throwing, pushing, carrying, or dropping, and in Jane's case that was the problem.

CHAPTER FOUR

RS. HILDRETH," SAID Jane. "I want to ask you a very, very serious question."

"Yes, dear?" said Mrs. Hildreth, putting down her scrubbing brush, and sitting back on her heels (in a puddle, although she didn't know it till it was too late). "What is it?"

"Have you been leaving out books for me at night?"

"No, dear," said Mrs. Hildreth, looking positively alarmed. Whatever was the child talking about?

"Cross your heart and swear to die?" said Jane, very severely.

"If you like, dear," said Mrs. Hildreth, quite

bewildered. She started asking questions at once, but she couldn't get anything sensible out of Jane.

As soon as she could get away, Jane ran off down to the beach to think.

Mrs. Hildreth had to go upstairs to change out of her wet dress, which didn't put her in the best of tempers. But later, when she'd stopped being cross with herself for sitting in puddles, she told Albert all about it.

"And just what do you make of that, Albert?" she said.

"Dunno," said Albert, looking under the stove for his pliers, although they were in the top pocket of his best jacket all the time.

"Oh, do stop and listen to me for once," said Mrs. Hildreth.

So he did.

"Well?" she said.

"I dunno, I'm sure, Maisie," he said, popping his head back under the stove to continue the pliers hunt.

Jane didn't get much help from the sea, but soon she saw a familiar face.

"Hullo," she said.

William Smollet tried to look down his nose at her, but as she was two inches taller than he was, he found himself looking up it, which wasn't at all satisfactory.

"Did she hit you?" he said.

"Who?" said Jane.

"When you got home?" he said. "Did she shout at you?"

"Of course not," said Jane.

"Oh," said William, feeling let down. In William's mind crime was clearly associated with punishment and there was something definitely wrong with a world where you didn't even get shouted at.

"Did you get into trouble?" said Jane.

"Oh no, of course not," said William, with his masculine dignity to consider.

"I'm glad," said Jane.

She wasn't really glad, but she badly

wanted someone to talk to about the books and the sweet smell, and William Smollet, ten-year-old battler that he was, was still the only person apart from the Hildreths that she knew to talk to in Rathard.

"Would you like me to buy you an ice cream?" said Jane, noticing that her audience was looking for a way to escape.

"I don't mind," said William, wondering what the catch was. He had to be careful. He did not want to be seen on the sea-front with a girl and yet he knew, *almost* for certain, that Nick, Addie, and Bopper were in the swimming pool and Sid had chicken pox and was covered all over with blisters. That meant that there was no one who could see him, or at least he hoped so.

"Thank you very much indeed," he said, taking the large ice cream.

They sat on the seawall and compared the size of the two lighthouses, the one on the pier and the Wreck Light on Hammer Island. The boats in the harbor were bobbing about wildly.

"That one," said William importantly, "is the lifeboat. They fire a cannon and it goes out and rescues people who are drowning."

"I know," said Jane, who had been told about it endlessly by Albert Hildreth. As coxswain of the lifeboat he thought lifeboats were a very interesting subject, and he often talked about them whether or not anyone was listening.

The conversation tailed off. William licked busily at his ice cream. Then he noticed that Jane had not bought herself one. He ought to offer her a lick of his but . . . *but* . . . if she had wanted an ice cream cone, she could have bought herself one, couldn't she? Yes. Undoubtedly. But, on the other hand, perhaps she hadn't enough money. Perhaps she had given away the very last of her money to buy him an ice cream. Well, in that case . . .

"Would you like a lick of my ice cream?" he said.

"There's none left hardly," said Jane, who had been waiting for him to suggest it, watching the ice cream grow smaller and smaller. Five pence was a lot of money to spend on an ice cream, and she was beginning to regret it.

"Don't take it all, will you?" said William anxiously, as Jane took the cone from him.

She broke off the bottom of the cone and divided the remainder of the ice cream equally.

"Thank you very much," she said.

"Not at all," said William, carefully inspecting his half to see that it *was* a half.

They finished the ice cream and William licked his fingers carefully clean, while Jane looked on disapprovingly, though she would have done the same thing if he hadn't been there. She felt that she ought to set him an example.

"Was it your very last penny you spent?" said William, who half hoped that, if it wasn't her last penny, she would buy him another one.

Jane didn't seem to hear him.

"Oh well," he said, hopping off the shore

wall, "must be going. I'm so busy these days you just wouldn't believe it." This is what Mrs. Smollet always said when she wanted to get away from people, and in her case it was often true, for the eight little Smollets and their father, Tobias, were quite a handful. It wasn't true in William's case, but he had had his ice cream, shared it, and said, "Would you like a lick of my ice cream?" and "Not at all," and it struck him that all that politeness was enough to waste on any girl.

"Wait a minute," said Jane, "I want to tell you a story."

William looked distinctly prune-faced. He had four older sisters. They were all very much inclined to take the four smaller Smollets and tell them stories. William was number five out of the eight and so he had heard the stories told to numbers six, seven, and eight as well as having his own turn. In his opinion he had heard every story in the world told at least four times, and that was three times too many.

"No, thank you very much," he said firmly. "I really must be on my way now. They will be wondering where I have got to." This again was what Mrs. Smollet always said, but this time it was true for William as well, because Nick, Addie, and Bopper probably were wondering where he'd got to. Two-a-side water polo is difficult to play when only three people have turned up, and William was late.

"*Please*, William," said Jane, sounding quite upset.

"Oh well," said William.

"I knew you would," said Jane, grabbing him before he could change his mind. She took a tight hold on his sleeve, just to make sure.

Then she told him her story, as though it was all happening to another little girl named Cynthia.

"And what do you think happened then?" she said, when she'd reached the bit about the sweet scent.

"They all lived happily ever after," said

William, impatiently. It was a very silly story in his opinion, and not at all the sort of thing he was used to. The four elder Smollet sisters had had plenty of practice and usually managed to put in blood and dragons and, on occasion, Tottenham Hotspur, so if he was tired of their stories, you can imagine how quickly he became fed up with Cynthia Something and her Mystery Books.

"Don't be silly," said Jane. "I want to know what happens next."

"Well, I don't," said William, wriggling free of her grasp. "If your story hasn't got an ending you can't expect me to tell you what it should be."

"But *supposing* it was real?" Jane said.

"Really must be going," said William, hopping over the seawall out of her reach. Then he ran away across the sand toward the swimming pool, where the Rathard Tigers Polo Squad was having a tough time without him.

Poor Jane.

William had not been helpful. Perhaps if he had realized that it was a true story, he might have paid more attention, but that didn't help Jane. She went home, or rather back to 3 Mole Street, which wasn't quite the same thing. There she asked Mrs. Hildreth for a rug and laid it out in the backyard where she promptly went to sleep in the sun.

"Well, I never," said Mrs. Hildreth, who had gone outside to fill the kettle from the yard tap.

The truth is that Jane had been awake most of the night, and with very good reason.

The Bracelets and *The Darlings of the Nations* were not very long books, and they had turned up in her room quite early. *The Phoenix and the Carpet* arrived well after midnight because Jane had made a determined effort not to go to sleep, and it was a much longer book. She finally finished it by reading under the bedclothes with her pocket flashlight, in case Mrs. Hildreth would see the light, and by then it was almost four o'clock.

No wonder she needed some sleep.

But that night, when Jane went to bed, she had her plans well laid. She was dying to know who or what was tricking her, and how the trick was done. It seemed . . . well, impossible.

So, first of all, she sniffed round the room, to see if she could catch any trace of the scent. Then she searched everywhere she could, looking for books. She tapped the walls and tested the floorboards looking for secret passages or hidden doors. Old houses often have such things, but there didn't seem to be any in Mole Street, which wasn't a hidden-room type of house anyway. She tried looking up the chimney, in case she could find the sort of steps boy chimney sweeps used to use hidden inside, but she got a faceful of soot for her trouble. Anyone who came down that was welcome to it.

"It must be a secret passage," she said, which was very puzzling, as she'd just decided that there weren't any secret passages. But the books weren't coming through the door, and they could scarcely have come through the window, unless someone was climbing up on a ladder from the outside, and somehow she couldn't see either of the Hildreths doing that.

It had to be done by someone who had books to lend and wore a nice sweet scent.

For a start that didn't sound at all like a secret-passage type person. She had a notion that secret passage people would wear high hats and cloaks and run around the place with kegs of gunpowder—and there weren't many like that in Rathard, though she supposed there might be just one, hidden away somewhere, forgotten about by his fellow conspirators.

By the time she'd finished searching she was very tired, but she took two more precautions before she finally went to bed. First of all, she took her talcum-powder tin and sprinkled a little powder round the floor, so that it would show footprints of anyone crossing the room. Then she pulled two hairs from her head—it hurt—and fixed one lightly across the catch on the door. The other one she laid on the join between the upper and lower parts of the window frame.

She went into a doze almost as soon as her head touched the pillow.

Later, something wakened her.

Was it . . . ?

She could hear nothing, but . . .

She sat up, and she was absolutely sure that she could smell something, the same delicate scent she had smelled before.

On went the light.

FIVE CHILDREN AND IT
by
E. Nesbit

The hairs were still in position when she inspected them, and the talcum powder on the floor was undisturbed.

 IVE CHILDREN AND IT kept Jane awake for a long time and the result was that she slept very soundly the following morning.

"She seems so tired," said Mrs. Hildreth. "I'll let her sleep it out, poor little thing."

Then she put on her coat and hat and went off up the hill to the farmhouse to lecture Mrs. Smollet about it.

"The kettle's on," said Mrs. Smollet wearily, "you'll stay and have a cup of tea, won't you, Maisie?"

"Not if it is too much trouble," said Mrs. Hildreth, settling herself in Tobias Smollet's rocking chair with every intention of having the tea she'd come for, too much trouble or not.

"Not a bit of trouble, Maisie," sighed Mrs. Smollet.

Then she called Kathleen, the eldest of her girls, to see to Barney and Sam, the Smollet twins, who were punching each other in the kitchen in the hope that with swollen noses and black eyes they would look as untwinlike as possible. Neither twin Smollet liked the look of the other one, so they set about the task with enthusiasm, apparently unaware of the danger all around them from steaming kettles and bub-bling pots.

"Out!" cried Kathleen, grabbing a twin in each hand and shoving them into the yard. She was tall and thin and overworked, for she had to do a lot of smaller-Smolleting, counting heads and keeping order, bandaging knees and clipping ears, and last, but by no means least, helping with homework. It sometimes seemed to Kathleen that there was no such thing as a holiday, for she was kept busy all the time, and it often seemed to the smaller Smollets that they could never have any fun without their big sister poking her nose in.

Back in the front parlor, Mrs. Hildreth was telling Mrs. Smollet about her problem with Jane, who wanted to sleep all day and, when she was awake, kept asking peculiar questions about books and wandering around the house as though she was looking for something. Mrs. Smollet listened patiently. With eight small Smollets of all sizes to cope with, she knew almost all there is to know about the-trouble-they-are-aren't-they dear, but it never crossed her mind to shut Mrs. Hildreth up by telling her so.

"Yes, Maisie," said Mrs. Smollet.

"No, Maisie," said Mrs. Smollet.

"I'm sure I don't know how you manage, Maisie," said Mrs. Smollet, with something very like a sigh of resignation.

Meanwhile in the backyard Barney and Sam Smollet had just lost Brenda, the smallest

Smollet, whom they were supposed to be looking after. William Smollet had fallen off the
roof of the barn and grazed his knee. Dora
Smollet had gone for messages and got lost
together with four pounds of sausages because
she saw a funny-looking butterfly and wanted
to catch it in her hat—which was a very special
hat. Lorna Smollet, the most beautiful of all the
Smollets, had decided she wanted to die
because of pimples—a new pimple had just put
in an appearance right on the tip of her beautiful nose. Bea Smollet, who should have known
better, had discovered that it is easier by far to
save up for a new pair of tights than to paint
your legs with brown gloss paint. Part of the
paint had come off all over everything and part,
despite urgent attention with a scrubbing
brush, persisted in staying on. Meanwhile,
Kathleen Smollet was searching the yard wondering which Smollet was crying, and where he
or she could be hidden. The angelic look on
Barney's face and the way in which he and Sam

tried to guide her away from the henhouse gave Kathleen cause for deep misgiving. Henhouses can be very mucky places and Brenda was not the sort of person who should be let loose inside one.

"One carries on as best one can," said Mrs. Hildreth, trying to look brave and careworn as she sipped her tea.

"Yes, Maisie," said the tiny Mrs. Smollet, who had much better things to be at, but didn't like to say so.

"Isn't that someone crying?" said Mrs. Hildreth, pricking up her ears as Brenda, turned into a chicken-manure baby, gave vent to her feelings. Her howls mingled with the cries of Barney and Sam as they met rough justice at the hands of Kathleen, who faced the prospect of washing her smallest sister from head to toe. "Is it?" said Mrs. Smollet, who had grown accustomed to the battle cries of her offspring over the years.

Mrs. Hildreth pursed her lips and tried not

to look too disapproving. If the Smollets had been her children, she thought to herself, she would have brought them up to be much better behaved.

"One worries," said Mrs. Hildreth, reverting to the problem that had brought her out to the farmhouse. "I can't think what I shall do to cheer the dear child up."

"Can't you?" said Mrs. Smollet, as the twin howls of Barney and Sam rent the air.

"What can I do?" said Mrs. Hildreth.

"Well, we usually hold surprise parties if we want to cheer someone up," said Mrs. Smollet.

"What a good idea," said Mrs. Hildreth.

And so . . .

at half past three . . .

there was a surprise party at 3 Mole Street, with eight Smollets, and the Carters, the Browns, Bopper Oviesky, and Hilda Dunlop suddenly arriving on the doorstep in a band to be greeted by a surprised—and still sleepy—Jane.

It wasn't a bad party, as parties go. Mrs. Hildreth, who liked things *just so*, had done her level best to make a fuss about having cakes that were bought and not homemade and about the absence of paper hats, but Mrs. Smollet, who was a sort of houseworking tornado, blew her aside and went resolutely on with the essentials. Between them they got together a lot of food, with Mrs. Hildreth doing the twiddly bits—carving each child's initials on the sausage rolls, for instance, while Mrs. Smollet made up monster sandwiches and, in between times, gave out instructions about everybody coming in old clothes so that disasters wouldn't matter.

And there were disasters.

Not all the Smollets had them. Kathleen was much too busy and self-important to be involved in such things and Lorna, who looked gorgeous despite her pimple (it was a gorgeous pimple), was fully occupied doing that and making sure she could see herself in every available mirror, from every conceivable angle. But the other Smollets made *small* mistakes, now and then.

It wasn't Barney's fault, for instance, that he fell down fourteen stairs and bruised his ribs; it was just the sort of thing that often happened to Barney—he was trying to throttle Sam at the time, so perhaps it served him right. Brenda didn't mean to spit out the jelly all over the carpet; she just didn't realize that the wobbly green stuff was jelly until she'd taken a bite. William and Bopper Oviesky did not intend to break the backyard tap and could not reasonably be held responsible for the flooding of the yard and the outside lavatory. Bea Smollet did not especially *want* to spill red ink all over Hilda Dunlop's best dress (which Hilda had insisted on wearing). Bea didn't mean to do it, but she wasn't really sorry that it had happened.

Only Dora Smollet could lay claim to an unqualified social success.

She came in her hat, of course, the one she wore in case she caught sunstroke. It was round and black and made of felt, and she said she had to wear it because of the sunstroke, but the truth is that Dora didn't need to wear the hat at all, and only said that she did because she liked wearing it. She kept things inside the lining, stamps and leaves—she liked leaves—and secret codes and the addresses of her best friends spelled backwards (Teerts Elom 3). She did her best to have her hat by her always and sometimes, secretly, wore it in bed. People said, "Why do you wear that ugly felt hat?" and Dora said, "I have to, because of sunstroke!"

Her moment of triumph came when Jane, who was hostess, shook hands with her politely and said, "I like your hat."

"So do I," said Dora, who was used to rough and ready Smollet rudeness, and thought that Jane meant it.

"It is most unusual," said Jane truthfully.

"I think it makes me look older," said Dora, "don't you?"

"Older than what?" said Jane, who thought

the hat was daft, and wasn't going to be caught that way.

"Than I am," said Dora.

Then they found that they were both the same age, almost exactly. Jane was born on the eighth of January and Dora on the twelfth, but then Dora had the hat and, as she pointed out, that made them almost equal. They talked about that, they talked about stamps, they talked about hockey, they talked about how awful William was and Dora, every so often, talked about her hat.

The really good thing about the party, as Mrs. Hildreth said later, was that it worked so well. Jane, who had obviously been fed up in Rathard, came right out of herself, and got on with Dora like a house on fire.

"I like Dora," Jane said to Mrs. Hildreth. "Do you know she has a complete set of Olympic Games Stamps?"

"Has she, dear?" said Mrs. Hildreth.

"And she says she'll swap me some," Jane

went on. Then she stopped and said, a shade sadly, "But I haven't got my stamps down here."

"No, dear," said Mrs. Hildreth.

"Do you think we could go to Belfast and collect my stamps?" Jane said hopefully. "It wouldn't take long in the car, and I could get some of my books as well."

"Now, don't be silly, dear," said Mrs. Hildreth. "In any case, you know your parents may be back quite soon."

"I hope they are," said Jane.

Mrs. Hildreth's face fell. She had tried very hard and Jane wished that she could have bitten her tongue out. "I did enjoy myself today," she said quickly. "You've been awfully good to me. But you do know what it's like. I miss them."

"Yes, dear," said Mrs. Hildreth, rather sadly. She had no children, and she knew that she never would have. She poked the fire and threw on another log. There was an uncomfortable silence while Jane tried to think of something to say to make up for her slip.

"I liked the girl with the smile," Jane said.

"Which one, dear?"

"Oh, the smiley one in the corner. I didn't speak to her, but she seemed to be enjoying herself."

"You should have made a point of speaking to all your guests, Jane," Mrs. Hildreth said.

"I suppose so," said Jane, who had been carried away with talking to Dora about Olympic Games Stamps. "I did try to get round to everyone, truly. But I didn't see her come in with the others and when I went to look for her afterwards she seemed to have slipped away."

"Must have been Hilda Dunlop," said Mrs. Hildreth, somewhat surprised. She would not have described the fat, overfed Hilda as "smiley" at all. Sour-faced was the right word.

"Oh, *no*, not *her*," said Jane. "I know who Hilda was. This one was quite different. She had a lovely blue velvet dress and a silk shawl, and black curly hair, and she seemed so happy.

All Hilda did was to sulk about the ink on her rotten clothes."

"Perhaps it was Lorna Smollet you saw," said Mrs. Hildreth.

But Jane knew that it wasn't. "The one I'm talking about was sitting over there in the corner on the stool," Jane said.

"What stool?" said Mrs. Hildreth.

There was no stool, no stool at all. Jane looked high and low for it. She looked all round the room, out in the hall, and in the kitchen. She would have looked in the yard as well, if Albert hadn't been wading around it in his lifeboat boots trying to fix the tap before the water level in the yard rose high enough to flood the kitchen. It was a small four-legged stool, and the girl had sat on it looking serious until she caught Jane's eye; then she clapped her hands and smiled, as if she wanted to show how much she was enjoying the company, and her little curls bounced up and down against her shoulders.

"She was about my age," Jane said. "I'd absolutely swear she was. And she was sitting on a stool, though goodness knows where it's gone to."

"That would be Bea," said Mrs. Hildreth.

But it wasn't Bea, and Jane knew it. Bea was the one with the dark-brown legs. Kathleen was the big bossy one. Lorna was the lovely one and the other likely Smollet was Dora, and it certainly wasn't Dora.

"I don't believe that my girl was a Smollet," said Jane. "She certainly didn't look Smolletish."

She said no more on the subject.

But she did remember something.

A girl seen from a distance, looking through the window of Jane's own room in 3 Mole Street, a girl with dark hair and a blue dress.

She didn't *want* to tell Mrs. Hildreth about it. The girl in the blue velvet dress was her mystery, part of the mystery of the books. She was determined not to tell anyone about it now, not even Dora Smollet, although Dora was her newly elected best-friend-in-Rathard. Whatever the explanation, she felt that it was something that lay between the two of them, herself and the smiling girl. It was their business, and nobody else's.

That night she didn't bother with the talcum powder and the hairs. She went to bed early, switched out the light, and waited.

Later, the book came.

HOW A YOUNG HOSTESS SHOULD BEHAVE

Notes on social etiquette for
young ladies about to enter society
by
Lady Clare Walloon
and *her friends*

Jane was left with the feeling that someone was trying, gently, to be helpful.

CHAPTER SIX

HE NEXT DAY it rained.

It was real Irish rain. It swept in from the sea and soaked down deep into the green of the estate, it started waterfalls in the quarry cuts on the mountainside, it sent a gurgling torrent down the middle of the High Street, and flooded the fields around the bog meadow. The sea roared and stormed and the wind whined and the roof of the kitchen started to leak so that Jane and Mrs. Hildreth spent a great deal of time rushing around with baking bowls and saucepans to catch the drips. When the storm eased a little they banked the fire high with turf blocks and settled in the back room where Albert told stories of

Shipwrecks He Had Known, and as Coxswain of the Lifeboat he had known rather a lot.

The stories didn't cheer Jane up much. After all, her own father and mother were due to sail back to Rathard any day in *The Seagull*, and she didn't like to think of them being drowned.

"But there haven't been many wrecks just here, have there?" she said anxiously.

"Depends what you mean by here," said Albert. "Many the one's gone adrift off this coast."

"Not just here, though," Jane insisted.

"Oh, I wouldn't say that, there's the Widows' Row down by the pier, you've seen that, I suppose? Houses put up for the widows after *The Eagle* went down in the bay. Then there was the rock boat that went down with all hands off Hammer Island, before they had the light there. Boss man and all, not a one came back from that trip."

"What's a rock boat?" said Jane, who had never heard of such a thing.

"A boat with rock from the quarries up the mountain beyond the town there. Oh, they're not worked now, but they used to use many a man up there—you can see the scars on the rock still. They'd quarry it up there and run it down on little trolley cars to the harbor, where it went off in boatloads to the big cities. Regular fine business it was, good jobs for a lot of men 'round here. The Quintons ran it. They were a grand family, had a hand in everything. Young Henry Quinton went down with his own rock boat, out there on Hammer rocks, and that put paid to the whole business in the end. The only good thing out of it was the light . . . . they put it up as a sort of memorial, to see the same thing wouldn't happen again."

It was not the sort of story that was likely to cheer Jane up.

That night she went to her room early, turned out the light, and said to herself, "I'd like to know more about the girl in the blue velvet dress."

It was a brave thing to do.

She lay in the darkness, waiting for something to happen. Twice now she had seen the girl, and she wanted to know more about her and the mysterious books. She had almost dozed off when . . .

She sat up and switched on the light.

On the bedside table lay a faded volume.

THE GIRLS' OWN PAPER
XXI
Illustrated
London 56 Paternoster Row

She had never seen anything like it. It seemed to be a whole year's weekly issues of a girls' magazine all bound together in one big book. There were all sorts of things in the weekly parts: household hints, articles about how to manage travel clubs and amateur dinners, how to make the oddest old clothes that no one could possibly want to wear. There were illustrations, too, pictures of girls playing tennis in ankle-length dresses with puffed sleeves, wearing the most ridiculous hats. . . . Dora might have liked them, but no sane person would. There was an article on *Cycle Gymkhanas: How to Prepare and Practice for Them,* by N. G. Bacon, with pictures of girls on bicycles having egg-and-spoon races and cycling 'round maypoles, somehow contriving not to tangle their long skirts in the chains of their odd high-saddled bikes. They had immense hats, too, piled high with flowers and ribbons.

Nineteen hundred was the year, as she found out from the dates on the magazines. She leafed through and looked at more of the articles. *Advice to Girls on entering Life's Battles. More About Peggy. Breadwinning at Home. A Few Hints on Repoussé Work. Cynthia's Brother. Her Sailor Lover: A Story of Sacrifice. Characteristic Church Towers of the English Counties.*

It was, to say the least, a very peculiar magazine, and not at all like anything Jane had ever seen in a shop. She plowed on. There was an

answer by the editor to a girl who had written
a letter asking about life at school: "Three
hours, from nine to twelve, could not be too
much at thirteen, unless a very delicate girl, in
which case special arrangements must be made.
She might attend again in the afternoon for a
couple of hours for music, art, or anything else."

That didn't sound much like school to Jane.

The very next answer from that editor was
to a girl who wanted to sell her hair. Jane had
never thought of that dodge either, although it
might be a way of getting book-buying money,
and she had more hair than she could use, especially when it got wet.

But that seemed to be all there was to the
book, and Jane laid it down with a distinct feeling that she had been cheated. She had hoped to
find out more about the girl, whoever she was,
but a bunch of old magazines from 1900 wasn't
much help. She was sure that the smiley girl
wasn't the type to play polo on a bicycle or sell
her hair to a hairdresser. It was just a silly old

book, and had nothing to do with anything. Up to now, the person providing the books had tried to be helpful, sending her E. Nesbit whom she liked, and then the social etiquette thing after she had not quite lived up to the job of hostess. This time, she'd been let down.

Or had she?

The book was old now, but it had been new once.

It had been someone's new book. All of them had been. *The Bracelets, The Darlings of the Nations*—someone had bought them, fresh and untouched in a bookshop, *once*. But the books were much older than the girl could possibly be. Then why should she have such old books? It was a riddle to which Jane could find no answer . . . at least no answer she could possibly allow herself to believe in. There was one answer, the obvious one, but she knew that it couldn't be *that*. Not in real life. There aren't any, are there?

She had asked for a book that would tell

her something about the girl in the blue velvet dress . . . did this one hold any clue? She went right through it again, but she couldn't find anything.

"I give it up," she said, putting the book down for the last time.

It was in the morning when the book had gone that she found the small white card which must have fallen from between its pages.

To M.
With lots of love,
Papa
Merry Christmas

Jane put the card out on top of her dressing table before she went down to breakfast, and she laid her tin of talcum powder on top of it, to make absolutely sure that it couldn't fall off or get blown away.

When she came back upstairs after breakfast, it was gone.

CHAPTER SEVEN

PICNICS ARE A splendid way of passing the time, at least seven of the Smollets thought so and Kathleen, who had to look after them while they were thinking it, didn't really mind picnics, although they were a lot of bother.

Seven of the Smollets, and Jane.

Dora came with the news first thing after breakfast, while Jane was still puzzling about the missing card.

"A picnic," said Jane. "Lovely."

But she didn't sound as though she thought it was lovely. She sounded as if her mind was on something else entirely.

"Of course you needn't come if you don't

want to," said Dora, tugging crossly at the side of her hat. It wasn't every day that people came running all the way downhill from their house to your house to tell you that they were inviting you to a picnic, and when it did happen you ought at least to dance around the room saying how wonderful they were, and how good and generous and kind.

"I should like to come," Jane said.

"Only *like?*" said Dora, who had gone to quite a lot of trouble getting Jane invited.

"Like very much," said Jane. "Thank you for asking me."

But later on, when she'd managed to get her mind off the mystery of the card, the books, and the girl in the blue velvet dress, she became much more interested in the picnic.

It was to be a Smollet-type picnic. That did not mean going forty miles in a motorcar to fry chicken in a rest area, not a bit of it. It meant making up lots of sandwiches with great thick hunks of cheese and fresh bread baked by Mrs.

Smollet. It meant sending out scouts to find early blackberries. It meant—unless someone kept an eye on William—that he was apt to disappear over someone's orchard wall and come back with large green apples which "just dropped at my feet, Kathleen." It meant going into the estate at the back of the town and beginning the long climb through the forests up the lower slopes of the mountain till you left the trees behind you and could see the whole town stretched out below. Then it meant plunging deep into the honey brown pools of the river and drinking fresh clear water and rescuing Brenda from the sheep she thought would eat her. It meant trekking in single file along the path where the quarrymen had once made their weary way to the workings. It meant climbing right to the top of Slievemore and putting stones on the cairn there, with your initials scraped on the underside.

It meant having a nice time.

"I like this," said Jane, although her legs were sore. She wasn't used to walking and climbing as the Smollets were, but she had done her level best to keep up, although Bea and Lorna kept running ahead on their long legs, and shouting impatiently at the others to hurry.

Jane and Dora were lying on a great flat rock above the picnic place, a rock from which they could see over the treetops to the roofs of the town, which seemed very small and far away, as though it were made of matchboxes. The harbor and the lighthouse had been laid neatly on the edge of a stretch of blue, and the little yachts and boats looked as though they had been tipped out of someone's bath.

"Why isn't it a proper harbor?" said Jane, who was used to watching great big boats come down Belfast Lough and thought that yachts and fishing boats, although they were pretty, weren't real boats at all.

"There's the *Ann Christie* and *The Harebell*," said Dora. She was talking about the boats that took tourists out to Hammer Island to see the bird sanctuary there.

"I mean boats like the ones that go to England," said Jane.

"You can't have everything," said Dora, who was rather proud of Rathard Harbor, and felt she had to defend it against all outsiders. "Those boats are too big for our harbor."

"Why?" said Jane.

"Because they draw too much water."

"What does that mean?"

"It means that our harbor isn't deep enough for them."

"For what?" Bea butted in, as she scrambled over the edge of the rock, having climbed up to it from the riverbed.

"Big boats," said Dora.

"I think there used to be big boats," said Jane. "I heard one of them got wrecked off Hammer Island."

"It can't have been very big," said Dora, who privately thought that she knew all there was to know about Rathard Harbor, and her sister Bea knew nothing. Bea might be the

Smollet who went out sailing with pimply Bob Agnew, but that didn't mean that she knew more about harbors than her seafaring sister. Dora thought of herself as a seafarer, something like Sir Francis Drake, only a girl.

She would not have been seasick in Ardglass Harbor like Bea.

She could have sailed single-handed across the Atlantic without turning a hair. The trouble was that Kathleen wouldn't let her, which was most unfair, and all because Kathleen fell out of a boat when she was six, and couldn't stand sailing.

"It's dangerous," Kathleen said, but Dora knew better. She had been for a secret sail on the boating lake at Newcastle and, although that wasn't quite the Atlantic, it was much the same thing, only smaller. After all, if you could row across the boating lake in Newcastle in ten minutes you had only to do a simple sum to see how easy it would be to row across the Atlantic. You had to divide the boating lake in

Newcastle into the Atlantic Ocean and multi-
ply the result by the time it had taken. Then
you had to add in time for breakfast, dinner, and
tea, and sleeping, and after that you knew
exactly how long it would take.

"Allowing for the current," said Jane.

"I would use the current to help me," said
Dora, who knew that was what real sailors
did.

"I shouldn't bother if I were you," said Bea,
who was busy inspecting the brown paint on
her leg, which was still a long way from all off.
"I doubt if you would get as far as Hammer
Island."

"I would not wish to do so," said Dora,
grandly. "Hammer Island is in the wrong direction. I wish to get to America, not Scotland."

They stood up to look at Scotland, which
they could just about see, a distant line of hills
on the horizon.

"It was a stone boat that was wrecked,"
said Jane, thinking back to Albert's story of the

lifeboat rushing out to Hammer Island, and the way it was forced back by the high tides that drowned every man on board. "There was no light on the island then, and she went on the rocks in the darkness," Jane said. "That's why there's a light now."

"I don't believe you," said Bea. "A boat made of stone would sink straight away."

"There are boats made of concrete," said Dora.

"I don't mean made of stone," said Jane. "I mean a boat carrying stone from the quarries. They used to run it down the mountain on a little railway thing. Albert says you can still see the tracks on the mountain where the trolleys ran."

"I wondered why they stopped," Bea said.

"I suppose people build with other sorts of stone now," Jane said.

"What a shame," said Dora, who felt that she could have had fun with little trucks rattling down the side of the mountain and being laboriously pulled back up it to the quarries. "I know," she said, "let's go back and see if we can trace the trolley tracks."

"Oh, I couldn't be bothered," said Bea, haughtily. She was certainly in no mood to spend all her time with two little nuisances.

But Jane liked the idea.

"You must be home by five-thirty," said Kathleen.

"No watches," said Dora, and she added, "unless you'd like to lend us yours?"

Kathleen wasn't having any of that. "You'll hear the clock strike, and not a minute after half past five, mind. And be careful not to go too far into the plantation."

Off they went.

They followed the quarrymen's path along the side of the mountain, till they found the beginning of the trolley rail, and a lot of old bolts and bars which they started collecting, found were too heavy, and threw away. The rails had been lifted, of course, but it was still easy to see the marks they had made on the rocks. They passed the east end of the planta-tion estate and then the line turned down and ran in a straight line toward the sea.

They soon got tired of following it, once the first interest of collecting bits and pieces had worn off.

The church clock struck three.

"If we go home now," said Dora, inspecting a sheep's skull she had found, "we shall be much too early."

"She did say five-thirty, and that's hours away," said Jane.

They looked at the track and they looked at the trees. The plantation looked exciting. It was a five-year-old planting of pine, which had been tagged onto the much older forest that stretched across the foot of the mountain.

"If we could find our way through the planting as far as the river, we could follow it down to Rathard House," said Dora.

"Kathleen said not to," said Jane, doubtfully,

for she didn't know the mountains or the estate,
and she was a little put off by the dark shadows
which played between the young straight
trees.

"Nonsense," said Dora, sticking her hat at
an explorer's angle. Then she was off, bobbing
and weaving among the trees, her feet sinking
into pine needles which spread like a springy
mattress between the trees.

When she got into the planting, Jane was
surprised at how strange she felt, for the sound
of their running feet was deadened by the pine
needles and the sun cut down through gaps and
lit up little grottoes and crannies which could
be seen a long way off. The trees, Jane thought,
made streets through the darkness, and she liked
going down the middle, heading straight for
one of the pools of light. Dora, who wasn't used
to streets and cities, didn't see it that way at
all. As far as she was concerned the trees were
for dodging among. It was a delicious leapy feeling to bound over the pine needles, to feel them

prick the soles of your feet, to be in there in the cool of the planting after the hours they had spent out on the blazing mountainside.

Then, quite suddenly, they came upon what had once been a path, which led them down into the older bit of the estate, away from the planting.

"Why, it's almost a road," said Jane, looking at the great stone cobbles laid on it.

"I wonder where it goes to?" said Dora.

They were both determined to find out.

The first remarkable thing they came to was a clearing filled with redwood trees, all twisted and turned into odd shapes, with huge branches springing out of the earth, so that you couldn't tell whether they were separate trees, or all part of the same one. The wood was soft to the touch, and the trees were grand for clambering about on.

"Let's go on," said Dora.

They went on, with walls of rhododendrons meeting over their heads, rhododendrons that sometimes blocked the path completely, so that they had to clamber over the branches and push aside the leaves and blooms till the path would clear again in front of them.

"I think we must be getting near the ruin," said Dora.

"What ruin?" said Jane.

But at that moment Dora slipped off the branch she was scrambling over and fell upside down in a mound of rotted leaves, so that she was much too preoccupied to reply.

The next thing they came to was not a ruin, however, but a very sturdy building, made out of the same sort of stone they had seen in the quarries. It was rather like a hermit's hut, but bigger, and open at one side so that the sun shone in on a great, round, tablelike stone. There was a stone ledge running 'round the side of the building which acted as a big seat. "It must be a summerhouse," said Jane, "a sort of picnic place. What a pity, we've already eaten ours."

They went inside and sat down on the ledge. The roof above their heads was made of sharp pointed stones with the sharp ends sticking downwards, so that it looked like a cheese grater. There were narrow windows set in the walls, like the arrow slits in Rathard Castle, but just a little bigger, as Jane found when she clambered up to explore them and found . . .

. . . a flight of little steps curving up on the outside of the summerhouse from the window.

She squeezed out through the window and battled her way up the steps through the undergrowth to find herself out on top of the building, which had a flat roof covered with grass.

"Jane?" said Dora.

"Up here," called Jane.

"Where's up here?" said Dora, who hadn't seen Jane slip through the arrow-slit window, and couldn't imagine how her friend had managed to disappear in broad daylight. She stepped out of the summerhouse onto the path.

"Up above you!" shouted Jane, standing by

one of the three stone horses that stood sentinel on the roof of the summerhouse.

"Goodness, how did you get up there?"

"Simple," said Jane, and she showed Dora the way up.

Together they stood on the roof, looking over the bushes toward the town.

"Look," cried Dora, pointing to the left. "There's Rathard House. I was right."And there it was indeed, gray stone walls rising up out of the undergrowth, flecked with ivy, with tree branches sprouting through the windowless gaps in the upper stories.

"This must have been their picnic house," Jane said.

"Race you!" cried Dora, and off they went, clambering down the steps, in through the arrow-slit window—more like a midget door, thought Jane, but still a window—and down the path. Jane was a good runner, but not so used to negotiating briers and brambles as Dora, and she came in a bad second, arriving in front of the ruined walls of Rathard House to find Dora hard at work picking raspberries.

"Nice, isn't it?" said Dora.

It was, in a funny way. It could have been miserable, many ruined old houses are, but it wasn't. It stood at the top of a slope which ran down to a high orchard wall, now completely overgrown. The place where the raspberries grew had been a terrace running round the house, where ladies and gentlemen must have walked, admiring the view of the sea. What had been a conservatory jutted out from the walls, weed and brier flowing over its rusting trellis work, dark browns and greens catching the light against the gray walls. Steel covers had been fixed over the doors and the roof had collapsed, but something of the air of elegance which Rathard House had once had still lingered. It made Jane think of ladies with parasols, and carriages rattling up the drives and . . . and chandeliers and things like that. Now it stood deserted, almost forgotten, in the midst of its own gardens, with its own estate stretching around it. The carriage drives were flooded with brier and bramble and tumbling walls of rhododendron, green and black shadows gored by summer pink and purple.

"What a lovely house," Jane said, a bit over-awed by it. How nice it must have been for the people who could afford to live in a great house like this one, with green wood all around them.

"Who lived here?" she said.

"Don't know," said Dora, in a matter-of-fact voice. She was used to flowers and trees and raspberries growing wild, and would have been much more impressed by Belfast Corporation Gasworks than the old ruin.

"I wonder what sort of people they were?" Jane said. Perhaps they would have been like the people in the *Girls' Own Paper*; men in evening suits, ladies in high hats decked with flowers, and fat little boys with ringlets.

They rambled around the building, skirting the terrace and finding their way onto a paved

walk, a sort of cloister, complete with pat-
terned paving stones, which had pictures of
peacocks and ladies in their nighties, shining
up through moss. As they came 'round the west
end of the house they heard the hum of the
river.

"How did it get like this?" Jane said, in a
half whisper, as if she were afraid that the own-
ers would hear her.

"Burned down in the war," said Dora. "But
it hadn't been lived in for years and years, as
far as I know." Then she said, "Race you!" and
darted off toward the river.

Jane did not pursue her.

She stood still.

Was it . . . ?

Yes, it was.

She turned and walked toward a smaller
ruined building, which might have been a coach
house, but she did not go in. Beside it there was
a wall, with an arched gateway, and a rusty
ornamental gate. She pushed it open—it had

been a kitchen garden, by the look of it, for the north side of the house swung 'round by it, and several steps at the far end led up to a barred doorway, which could have opened into the kitchens, or the servants' quarters. The garden might have been for vegetables, or flowers.

Now it was filled with wild lavender.

Lavender.

There was an overgrown fountain and the frame of a greenhouse, half of which had collapsed. She walked toward it, but a huge bramble stopped her. She turned aside and picked some lavender to take with her.

Lavender. The sweet smell in her room had been lavender.

She left the garden, closing the rickety gate behind her, and ran 'round the coach house toward the chattering of the river, where Dora waited impatiently on the bridge.

"What kept you?" she said.

"I like that house," said Jane.

The church clock struck five.

"What do you want that for?" Dora said, pointing at the bundle of lavender in Jane's hand.

But Jane didn't tell her.

CHAPTER EIGHT

HAT NIGHT SHE saw the girl in the blue velvet dress again.

Jane had put the lavender in a pretty jug and placed it on the sill of her window, where she felt sure it would be seen.

After tea she went up the hill to see Dora, for they had decided to go out on the *Ann Christie* to Hammer Island the following day, and wanted to plan the expedition.

It was late when Jane got back and she was tired and ready for bed. She tramped wearily upstairs and opened the door of her room.

The girl was standing by the window, look-ing at the lavender, her small white face solemn.

"Hullo," Jane said bravely.

The girl turned slowly, gave a small smile . . .

. . . and disappeared.

So she *was*, wasn't she?

CHAPTER NINE

RS. SMOLLET WAS doing the washing. In most households that means some disruption, and there are only two or three people in most households. Mrs. Smollet had to do the washing for eight young Smollets and Tobias, as well as her own, and you might think that a Smollet washday would be a very disorderly operation, but in fact it wasn't.

With so many pairs of underpants and so many dirty socks, it had to be well organized.

Mrs. Smollet and Kathleen chased Barney and Sam out, locked Brenda in with a grumpy Bea to look after her, and made certain that the lovely Lorna had got all her beautiful dirty things into the wash, a thing the lovely Lorna wasn't all that careful about.

Then they put several pots full of water on the stove, prepared the washtub, got out the soap powder and . . .

"Good morning, dear," said Mrs. Hildreth, "I'm not interrupting when you're busy, I hope?"

"Not at all, Maisie," said Mrs. Smollet with a sigh, leading her friend out of the kitchen.

Kathleen didn't sigh, she was furious, and said a number of things to her transistor set that no well-brought-up Smollet should have said—luckily the transistor was made in Japan and couldn't understand a word. She went upstairs to look for the lovely Lorna, in the hope that the second-eldest Smollet might help.

"Can't," said Lorna.

"Why not?" said Kathleen.

"Washing gives me a rash. You know how delicate my skin is."

"Then what are you going to do when you get married?"

"I shall have butlers and maidservants," said Lorna, carefully combing her hair.

"People don't have butlers anymore."

"In that case," said Lorna grandly, "I shall make do with a washing machine." She closed the door of the room firmly in her sister's face, and lay down to take her afternoon beauty sleep. She was, after all, going to be a film star and support the whole family on her fabulous earnings, and she was already fourteen. At eighteen, she had decided, she would go to Hollywood and ask for a screen test. After that . . . well, beautiful clothes, rich men, and a life of idle luxury. Which was why it was important to look after her complexion *now*, washing or no washing.

"Spoiled!" Kathleen shouted through the door, but she had to do the washing alone.

Meanwhile, in the front room, the cause of all the bother was explaining yet another of her problems to Mrs. Smollet.

"And then, whatever do you think the child said?"

"I haven't the least idea, dear," said Mrs. Smollet patiently.

"'Do you believe in ghosts?' That's what she said," said Mrs. Hildreth.

"Yes, dear."

"Do you?" said Mrs. Hildreth, taken aback.

"No, dear."

"But you said, 'Yes, dear.'"

"No, dear, I didn't."

"But . . . oh, never mind," said Mrs. Hildreth. "That's what Jane said anyway, and I'm sure I don't know what to make of it. She seemed to be so serious about it."

"Yes, dear," said Mrs. Smollet, automatically.

"So I said 'no,'" said Mrs. Hildreth, "and do you know what she said?"

"No, dear," said Mrs. Smollet.

"'I think you're quite wrong,' that's what she said!"

"Well, I never," said Mrs. Smollet, who had just remembered that she'd put the starch in an old soap packet and was wondering if . . .

* * *

"Ghosts are silly," said Dora. They were sitting on a bench outside the Wreck Light, which was much bigger than the lighthouse in the harbor.

"I don't think so," said Jane who, after all, *knew*.

"And scary," said Dora.

"Oh, no, they're not," said Jane.

"How do you know?"

But Jane wasn't going to give away her secret. "I just know," she said.

"Skeletons and bones," said Dora, carefully inspecting her hat to see if all the things she kept inside it were intact.

"Ghosts aren't like that at all," said Jane.

"What are they like then?" Dora challenged.

"Like you and me, only different," said Jane.

Dora didn't seem to think much of that as an explanation.

"A ghost I know of," said Jane carefully, "a

ghost that appeared to a friend of mine wasn't at all like that."

"What was it like?" said Dora. "Was it a headless horseman in chains?"

"No."

"Or covered in blood and crying, 'I will not rest e'er I be revenged'?" said Dora, who had read a lot of ghost stories.

"This was a sort of cheerful ghost," said Jane. "Well, not cheerful all the time, but sort of friendly, anyway."

"Hmmh!" said Dora, who privately thought that the whole conversation was silly.

"Not cheerful all the time," said Jane, thinking of the small sad face of the girl as she stood looking at the lavender in her room, "but sometimes cheerful, do you see what I mean?"

"No, I don't," said Dora, scrambling to her feet, "and I don't particularly want to see either."

"Do listen, Dora," said Jane. "What I want to know is this: would a ghost enjoy things that we enjoy, like, for instance, a party? I mean just supposing that a ghost somehow turned up at a party, would it enjoy itself, just as if it was one of us?"

"A real ghost would be one of us, if there were such things," said Dora.

"But a ghost is a ghost," said Jane.

"If a ghost is the ghost of a dead person, it stands to reason they've been alive, doesn't it?" said Dora impatiently. "I don't think that being supposed to be dead makes much difference to parties, do you? Perhaps your ghost doesn't even know she is dead."

"My friend's ghost," said Jane quickly.

"I don't care whose ghost it is," said Dora. "I should think ghosts are pretty much like us really, except that we can do something about what happens to us, and they more or less have to put up with what they've got. Not," she added quickly, "that I believe in ghosts, anyway."

"Of course not," said Jane.

They went back to the *Ann Christie* and were almost last on board so that Harry Dougan, who ran the boat, shouted at them and made them run. They arrived in a terrible state, and were bundled into their seats.

"Sitting up by the Wreck Light jawing," grumbled Harry.

As the boat ran across the narrow channel that separated Hammer Island from the mainland, Jane sat with her hand in the water and thought about her ghost.

Did the girl in the blue velvet dress know that she was dead?

It would be awful to be dead, and not know it.

On the other hand, Jane knew that people were supposed to be scared of ghosts, and she couldn't for the life of her feel scared of her ghost, who was more like a friend. Of course, they had books as a common interest, and that was a start. "Maybe that's why she picked on me to appear to," Jane thought, but she had a notion that there might be more to it than that.

Why shouldn't the girl enjoy parties, even if she was a ghost?

A party is a party, Jane decided. Then she had another idea. Perhaps the ghost was lonely! That would account for her happiness at the party, seeing so many people of her own age. "What a nice idea," she thought, and she resolved to make an extra-special effort when she got home to show the girl in the blue velvet dress that she, at least, was not afraid to keep a lonely ghost company.

Perhaps all the girl needed was a friend.

She was determined to put it to the test.

"Sleepy, dear?" said Mrs. Hildreth.

"Very," said Jane, with an exaggerated yawn.

"The sea air, I suppose," said Mrs. Hildreth, but she was wrong.

Jane climbed the stairs quickly and went

into her room. Then she sat down on the bed and waited.

Nothing happened.

"I want to be friends," she said, "I want to help you if I can."

Still nothing.

"Oh, come on," she said, "do show yourself. I'm not frightened, truly."

Still nothing happened.

She lay back on her bed. She felt she ought to do something to help her ghost, but she wasn't at all sure what it was to be. After all, the ghost must need help, or she wouldn't keep appearing, would she? But all the appearing and smiling in the world didn't add up to much if Jane was still left with no idea of what the girl in the blue velvet dress wanted her to do. She could, of course, have written to her father and mother to ask them what they thought, but she couldn't be sure where they were, because they were touring around studying rock strata in the Highlands. Mr. Reid's work as a geologist often took him into odd and unexpected places; it was something they had learned to put up with. Obviously the postcard she had sent them, c/o Uncle Tom, hadn't reached them yet, and there was no guarantee that a letter would either. And even if it did, what on earth could she say in it?

> *Dear Daddy and Mummy,*
> *I have met a ghost.*
> *Love, Jane.*

The fact is that most people don't meet ghosts, or if they do they keep very quiet about it . . . although it is possible that people meet ghosts and don't know it, of course.

The only person she could ask to help was Dora, and she already knew what Dora thought about ghosts. She liked Dora, she liked all the Smollets, in one way or another, even William, but they weren't the sort of family who would give good advice on how to help a ghost sort out her problems.

"I'm sure she wants me to help," Jane thought, "I'm *positive* that that's why she keeps appearing to me."

But the best person to ask about it was the girl in the blue velvet dress herself! "Of course," Jane thought, and she hurried off downstairs to fetch a pencil and paper.

"What?" said Albert, who had just turned the sofa upside down to get at the broken springs.

"Have you a pencil, please?" Jane said.

"Hold that for me, would you, Jane?" he said, and the next moment Jane found herself propping up the far end of the sofa while Albert got hotter and crosser working inside it, cursing springs and fluff which seemed to fly out over everything.

It was half an hour before she finally got back upstairs, leaving an exhausted Albert who had by this time succeeded in getting the sofa stuck in the frame of the back window in an effort to move it out into the yard. Quite how

long it was going to be there was a question to
which even Albert did not know the answer,
for he had had to send out for four of his friends
to help him shift it. Meanwhile the window
which he had taken out lay against the yard
shed, and the rain, which had just come on
heavily, beat down upon the sofa and, through
the space where the window had been, on the
rest of the Hildreths' furniture.

"I shall have to saw up the sofa," said Albert.

"You can't do that!" cried Mrs. Hildreth, in
distress.

"In that case," said Albert, "I shall have to
knock down the wall, or leave it sticking where
it is."

There were perhaps some advantages in liv-
ing in modern bungalows with fancy furniture
and, at that minute, even Mrs. Hildreth would
have admitted it.

Up in her room, Jane had settled down on a
chair, by the window, to write her letter to the
ghost.

To: The Ghost (M),   From: Miss J. Reid,
3 Mole St.,   3 Mole Street,
Rathard.   Rathard.
September 3rd

Dear Ghost,

Thank you very much for my books. I enjoy
E. Nesbit particularly, which is why you lent it, I
suppose. I would like to read The Railway Children
again if you have it. It was on television. Did
you see it?

Well, ghost, I am writing this to see if there is anything I can do to help you, as you have been so nice to
me. Ghosts are supposed to be unhappy and, although
you seem quite happy usually, I would like to know if
you are unhappy and if I can help.

My name is Jane Reid and I live at 5 Ormeau
Bungalows, Gallowley, Belfast, Ireland.

What is your name? Did you live here once? Did you
live in Rathard House before it was burned down?
Are you sad? Is there anything I can do?

(She stopped to think for a bit, then she
went on.)

Are you "M"? What does "M" stand for?
Was that card from your Papa?

(She used the word Papa, although it
seemed odd to her, so that the ghost would
know whom she was talking about.)

Well, ghost, that is all I have to say now. I hope
you are keeping well and don't mind being a ghost
too much. I like your dress and your hair is
very shiny.

Lots of love,

Jane

XOXOXOXOXOXO

She inspected the letter very carefully, then
she read it through twice for spelling, and
finally added a footnote.

P.S. Do you read a lot of books too?

She considered this deeply, being not at all

sure whether, when addressing a ghost, one ought to write "Do you read a lot of books?" or "Did you read a lot of books?" She settled for "do" because "did" seemed somehow insulting.

She folded the letter up, with a sprig of lavender inside it, and left it propped up against the windowsill. Then she went off downstairs to see how they were getting on with the sofa.

Jane didn't get any farther than the hall, where she heard Tobias Smollet's voice saying, "I think we should take the kitchen door off its hinges, Albert."

"I can't see how else we can move the stove, Maisie," said Albert, "and if we don't move the stove, we shan't be able to get the sofa out through the kitchen, will we?"

"Then leave it in!" said Mrs. Hildreth, sounding exasperated.

"But you wanted it taken out," said Albert crossly. "You said the fluff was getting all over the sitting room."

What Mrs. Hildreth said then caused Tobias Smollet and his two friends to leave in a hurry, and they were ex-members of the Merchant Marine, who had been around the world.

It also sent Jane hurriedly upstairs again, wondering what on earth those words meant. She did ask Mrs. Smollet later, but Mrs. Smollet didn't seem to hear her.

The note had not been moved. It lay on the windowsill, exactly where she had left it.

"Perhaps I'm imagining it all," Jane thought. "Perhaps I dreamed all those books, and just thought I saw the girl. It might be some sort of mirage." That didn't sound right though . . . surely mirages happened at sea, and in the desert, not in people's bedrooms?

Could she have imagined complete stories, like the ones in the books?

She undressed and went to bed. Then she switched off her bedside lamp and waited.

No ghost.

She closed her eyes and tried to go to sleep.

Then she opened them again, took a look to see if the note was there (it was), and lay back again.

"Please, please try to tell me how I can help you, ghost!" she said to herself. Perhaps there was a secret passage, and treasure, or a sorrowing parent to be told. Perhaps . . . but it was all a bit creepy.

"Please, ghost," she said, out loud.

She lay on and on and grew sleepier and sleepier and then . . .

Lavender. A sweet scent of lavender.

She sat up, but she didn't switch on the light.

"Are you there?" she said. "I'm not frightened, truly I'm not. I want only to help you, if I can."

There was no sound.

"I thought you might be afraid of the light," she said. "So I won't switch it on if you don't want me to."

No sound.

"I left a note on the windowsill."

At that moment someone tapped on the door!

A ghost is a ghost is a ghost.

Jane was quite prepared to meet a lavender-smelling ghost who drifted around the house like a sort of extra-quiet library assistant, but she hadn't bargained for a door-tapping one.

Under the bedclothes she went.

"Jane, dear, are you all right?"

"Yes, Mrs. Hildreth," said Jane, greatly relieved, pulling the bedclothes back.

"And I could have sworn I heard the child talking to herself," Mrs. Hildreth said, when she got back downstairs, but Albert Hildreth just said, "Oh yes?" and went on scowling at the sofa, which had no right to be a not-going-through-narrow-windows shape.

Half an hour later Mrs. Hildreth went upstairs to ask Jane if she *had* been talking to herself, but the room was still dark, and Jane had gone to sleep.

"I won't disturb the child," Mrs. Hildreth said, and she went off to bed.

It was much later when Jane woke up. She lay in bed blinking in the soft light from the gas jet, and wondering why she felt so odd.

Gas jet.

She sat up at once and looked around her.

The room had changed.

The walls were lined with brown book-shelves, and the shelves were filled with books. All shapes, sizes, and sorts of books: some bound in dark leather, others with ornate gilt lettering, and others . . . oh, books of every imaginable sort, lining the room from floor to ceiling.

It *was* a dream.

She decided this at once, because she knew that the Hildreths' little room was a gleaming buttercup yellow and filled with white things. The room she now lay in was book-colored in the gleam of the gas jet, all browns and reds and purples hazing together, with heavy red drapes pulled across the window. There was a table and an armchair with a padded leather back that looked very comfortable, and a pipe rack sat on the table filled with pipes of all shapes and sizes, some of them cunningly carved, so that they looked like pistols, or barking dogs, or old seamen with white ivory eyes.

Jane decided that, as dreams tend to come and go, she had better get out of bed and make the most of this one while it lasted.

She felt her way through the darkness to the lighted corner of the room where the gas hissed merrily and as she moved, the arc of light seemed to grow out around her, until it almost filled the room. She looked back at the corner she had come from, but it was all in darkness. She could not see her bed.

"How peculiar," she said to herself, but she put it down to being in a dream.

Books!

Charles Dickens, Walter Scott, Captain

Mayne Reid, E. Nesbit, Gordon Stables, R. D. Blackmore, Andrew Lang, Rosa Nouchette Carey, Evelyn Everett Green, Charles Lever, Somerville and Ross, Charles Kingsley, Frederick W. Farrer, Frances Hodgson Burnett, Alexander Dumas, Plato, Sheridan Le Fanu, and . . . oh, lots more, some she had heard of and some she hadn't. There were lots of the big bound magazine books, like the *Girls' Own Paper*. She saw *Sunday at Home, Our Own Gazette, Every Girl's Annual*, and a lot of others. There were books she didn't like the look of at all, like *A History of Great Temperance Reforms* and *Emblems for the Young from Scripture, Nature and Art* by the late Cornelius Neale, M.A. (which had lots of nice woodcuts, but very little else). There were books which had odd names like *Retiring from Business* and *Timothy Titcombe's Letters to Young People* and *Friends and Foes in the Transkei, An Englishwoman's Experiences During the Cape Frontier War of 1877-8*. There were . . .

Books.

Books galore.

She settled down in the padded chair to read *Underground London*, which sounded exciting at first, but turned out to be about sewers, and so she went on to *Eric, Or Little by Little*, a big fat blue book which took quite a long time to finish.

So long, indeed, that she could hardly keep her eyes open toward the end.

"Finished," she said, putting the book in its place, and almost falling off the little library steps with tiredness as she did so. The steps were small and had green felt padding on each tread, and she would have liked them for her own room at home to help her reach the high shelves. She would have liked the whole room for her very own, and she wanted to stay on in the dream and read more but . . .

She was so tired, and the gaslight seemed to grow dimmer around her, and suddenly she felt that she had to get back to bed *at once*, before she fell asleep on her feet.

Jane moved carefully into the dark corner she had come from, and away from the table and the chair and the bookshelves and the rapidly fading light from the gas jet. Across the room—somehow it seemed to be a long, long journey—until her knees struck against the bed, and she sank down upon it.

A moment later she fell sound asleep, which is a curious thing to do in the middle of a dream.

CHAPTER TEN

HE SKY WAS black and stormy, and the sea beat upon the front wall and showered spray over the two small figures huddled in the bus shelter, waiting for the 11:30 to Kilport.

"I like storms," said Dora, keeping a firm grip on her hat, in case it should blow away.

They moved to the far side of the shelter, away from the spray, and the lady in the yellow suit went racing by in her car and soaked them all over again as she squealed 'round the Post Office corner in a cloud of spray.

"Oh, look!" said Jane, scraping some mud out of her eye.

"Mrs. Carew always drives like that," said

Dora. "I don't suppose she ever took a driving test, do you?"

"No," said Jane, but her mind wasn't really on the demon driver of Rathard. She was still wondering about the bookroom. Was it a dream or was it, well . . . something else altogether?

After all, if she was prepared to believe in a ghost, why not a ghost room as well? Perhaps the girl in the blue velvet dress had once lived in the room, with her books?

Most little girls don't smoke pipes.

Suppose . . .

She had had her supposing interrupted when Dora arrived, complete with slicker and hat, and bursting with self-importance.

"I've got to go to Kilport on a Secret Mission," Dora announced importantly. "Don't you want to come?"

So off they went.

"What sort of Secret Mission?" said Jane, as they stood in the shelter trying to clean off the mud which Mrs. Carew's mad driving had shot all over them. The wind buffeted them hard and caught at the bushes on the promenade, bending them in toward the land. It tangled seaweed in the telegraph wires and made the "Bed and Breakfast" signs swing wildly to and fro. It was certainly not a day to be at sea, Jane thought, with a little shiver.

"A Secret Mission on behalf of Brenda, William, Barney, and Sam," said Dora. "I am sworn to eternal silence."

"But you'll tell me?"

"It was pain-of-death, but I suppose I will," said Dora, who was dying to tell someone. "I don't think you count on that particular swear, not being a Smollet."

The bus came 'round the station wall and down the sea front, its windshield wipers working furiously. When Jane and Dora climbed on board they found that all the seats had been filled by large ladies with shopping baskets and dogs, each and every one of them wrapped in slickers and rubber boots. From each and every one of them rose a small cloud of steam as they dried out in the stuffy atmosphere of the bus.

"You'd think that they were all on fire," said Dora, and they certainly looked it, with their cheeks blazing red and their wet hair blown free of their waterproof hoods looking like wisps of gray smoke.

"Your Secret Mission?" Jane prompted.

It was a Secret Birthday-Present-Buying Mission. The four smaller Smollets and Dora had clubbed together and raised fifty-three pence for Mrs. Smollet's forty-eighth. One from Brenda, who was the smallest Smollet of all, ten pence from Barney and Sam, twenty pence of hard-earned paper-round money from William, and the remainder from Dora—the profits from a stamp sale to Hilda Dunlop which almost ended in a fight. By Smollet standards fifty-three pence was incredible riches. Dora, as the eldest of the quintet, was ordered to spend it wisely.

Kilport, when they got there, proved to be only a little bit bigger than Rathard itself. It had a harbor, but no lighthouse. There were four main streets of shops which, in Dora's mind, put Kilport second only to Piccadilly as a shopping center.

Jane didn't think much of the shops. She was used to Marks & Spencer and Woolworths and inclined to be a little stand-offish about "Hill's General and Hardware" and "Dolores McGuigan Fashion of Paris Inc.," although she fell in love with the gleaming brass change-railway that ran around the ceiling inside Breen's Grocery. The assistants put change and bills into little metal tubes and pulled a lever, and off the tubes went, rattling 'round the shop on shiny rails. Breen's wasn't exactly a present shop, although they did consider seriously a large tin of biscuits with a picture of a house on it. "But we'd eat them all ourselves," said Dora sadly, for she would have enjoyed eating them.

They looked in the windows of "McCall's

Cash Drapery" and the "Coke, Iron and Steel Company," but they didn't see anything that looked at all hopeful.

Then they came to the Market Square.

It was packed.

The fat ladies from the bus were everywhere, swooping around the stalls, lifting old petticoats and nonstick pans, slapping cross children, arguing about prices, bulk-buying once-only offers of cornflakes (seven packs for twenty pence) and soap—there was one stall completely covered with big green blocks of soap, with the dirtiest man in the world selling it.

"Well, I wondered where they'd all got to!" Jane exclaimed.

She thought she was saying it to Dora, but she wasn't. Dora had disappeared into the crowd, somewhere east of the large black bottoms and shopping bags, west of the carrots and cauliflowers, and in between the old evening dresses and the red, white, and blue parkas, the pet rabbits, and the pop records.

"I don't think much of that," said Jane stiffly.

She did start looking for Dora, but it was a hopeless task and she soon gave it up.

There were much more interesting things to look at.

Junk stalls. A man selling a fruit-cutter, who bawled nonstop at the top of his voice. A man with dolls that danced. He held a board before him and when he tapped it their wooden knees and elbows jigged up and down. A man with cheap chocolates. A man with eiderdowns, who was giving them away—almost, but not quite. A man with onions. A fat lady with piles of pink and blue corsets, and last, but by no means least, a man with a face like a carrot who stood by a washbasin full of books.

Jane caught sight of him just as he was packing up for the day. He stood some way back from the crowd and had begun to pack his books back into the battered baby carriage in which he had brought them.

Books.

"One penny each," he said, as she bent down to look at them.

They were a disappointment.

Even one penny was a bit much for *A Junior Greek Primer* or *Smith on Kidneys* (which had some horrible pictures inside it). Jane rummaged on through the pile.

"Hurry up," said the man, "I'm going home, soon as you've finished."

"Don't let me keep you," said Jane, standing back, because she was more than a little afraid of the market people, who seemed to be so full of bustle and business.

Then she saw it.

"Oh!" was all she could say.

"I've got it," cried Dora, "absolutely the most beautiful present anyone ever had!"

Jane settled on the bus seat beside her. She, too, had got something from her expedition, but she didn't mean to talk about it.

"Don't you want to know what I've bought?" said Dora, patting the large round box on her knee.

"Yes, please," said Jane politely, although she was much more interested in her own discovery.

"There!" exclaimed Dora, throwing back the lid of the box. "Don't you think that is positively the loveliest, most gorgeous thing you have ever seen?"

Jane looked into the box.

She saw what looked like a plastic pear, some green leaves, some dirty white plastic flowers, and half a pineapple.

"What is it?" she said, feeling just a bit stupid.

"Don't be silly," Dora said, "it's a hat!"

And she scooped it up out of the box and displayed it proudly.

It *was* a hat, but only just. It was large and floppy and made of stiff green and yellow straw, with all the bits and pieces of plastic fruit and flowers stitched onto the top of it. Sweetpea, honeysuckle, daisies, grapes—it looked to Jane as though someone had upturned a heap of garden refuse on top of the hat and left it there, before anyone could fine them ten pounds for dumping. It was probably the ugliest hat she had ever seen.

"Isn't it just scrumptious!" said Dora, putting it on her head. It was much too big, and it slipped down over her eyes.

A lady two seats back nudged her friend and laughed.

"What a day for a fancy-dress parade!" said someone.

Jane thought they were being most unkind, but fortunately Dora didn't realize the effect she was making, probably because her eyes and ears were covered by the hat. "So much lining, too," she said happily. "I could keep anything in there, if it was my hat."

"Does your mother keep things in the lining of her hats?" said Jane, doubtfully.

"She never wears hats," said Dora.

There was a dreadful silence while they thought about it.

"She'll wear this one though," Dora said, "won't she?"

They both looked at the hat.

"Y-e-s," said Jane untruthfully. She had to say *something*. A lot of people had noticed the hideous hat now, and several of them were sniggering at Dora, who had propped it up on her ears.

"*You* would wear it if it was *yours*, wouldn't you?" Dora said. Then she added, confidently, "I expect you'd never have it off your head."

"It is very nice," said Jane, dodging the question. The thought of little Mrs. Smollet parading around Rathard with an entire botanical garden on her head convinced Jane that Dora had made a mistake, but she didn't want to be the one to break it to her. Dora was the only real friend Jane had in Rathard (apart from the ghost) and, if Dora was mad about hats, Jane would just have to be mad, too.

"I tell you what," Dora said, "I shall let you wear it until we get to Rathard," and with that she set the hat on Jane's head, where it slid gently over her ears.

Somebody tittered.

"What an odd little girl," said someone else.

"It does look lovely," said Dora approvingly.

Jane sat where she was, uncomfortably aware of the awful thing on her head.

"The mad hatter!" said someone, and a ripple of laughter spread around the bus, as the large wet ladies enjoyed the joke.

"I think, if you don't mind, that I'll just slip it off now," said Jane.

"But I *allow* you to wear it till we get to Rathard," said Dora, who thought that her friend was being bashful. She had never seen anything so lovely as the hat. She knew it *had* to be her mother's birthday present the moment she saw it in the market. Everything else on the old-clothes stall paled into insignificance beside the hat. She picked it up from among the other old things and fingered it gently.

"Please don't handle the goods," said the stallholder, a great fat woman with a ferret face, who didn't want to waste her time with little girls who had no money.

"But I would like to buy it," Dora said.

"Would you indeed?" said the woman, in amazement. She couldn't think what anyone could want with the wretched thing. "Beautiful hat, that is," she said. "Posh. I could fancy it for myself."

"Isn't it nice?" Dora said, glad to have her judgment confirmed. Then she thought to herself, "If it's a posh hat, it will cost pounds," and she wondered nervously if the woman could possibly be persuaded to accept fifty-three pence for such a beautiful and marvelous creation as the fruit hat.

"How much is it?" she faltered at last.

The woman was about to say, "Thirteen pence to you," but she stopped herself just in time and said: "How much have you got, dearie?"

"Fifty-three pence," said Dora, truthfully.

"Well," said the woman, frowning, "it cost me almost that, you know. I was looking for at least two pounds."

"Oh," said Dora, letting go of it.

"But seeing as it's you," the woman said quickly, "I dare say I can let you have it for fifty-three pence, though why I'm throwing money away I'm sure I don't know."

Then she shot the hat into its box and thrust it at Dora, half afraid that her customer might change her mind. "Don't you go telling your Ma and Da what you paid for it," she said. "I dare say they'd come rushing here demanding bargains if they knew how generous I am."

"Oh, I won't," said Dora, "I promise."

So it was that Dora bought the hat, which Jane had quietly slipped off her head and laid on the seat across the aisle from her.

They drove along in silence, watching the sea break on the rocks. Then the bus pulled to a stop, just outside Rathard.

"It doesn't usually stop here," said Dora. "Oh, my goodness, look!"

The largest hiker in the world, complete with the biggest knapsack and the shortest shorts, was squeezing his way onto the bus. He must have weighed at least 250 pounds, and his shaggy hair mingled with his beard so that hardly any face could be seen—just a big blue nose and hair. He had a frying pan and a kettle which hung from the back of his knapsack and he was drenched to the skin, despite his professional-looking slicker of yellow plastic and his little yellow hat.

He staggered up onto the bus and sat down just across the way from the girls.

"Wheeh!" he said, shaking himself like a dog, so that the water from his hair sprayed over everyone in range.

"Isn't he wet?" said Dora cheerfully.

Jane had gone pale.

"Isn't he wet, Jane?" said Dora again.

Jane looked at the hiker, and she looked at Dora. Her friend had evidently not heard the terrible crunching sound when the largest, hairiest, and wettest hiker in the world sat down.

"Where did you put the hat, Jane?" asked Dora.

And Jane told her.

A squashed plastic pear.

Several screwed-up grapes.

A pile of flattened daisies.

A broken-down half-pineapple which had burst.

A mass of green straw and a splendid lining.

The best hat in the world would not have stood much chance against the large back-side of Hermann Gotheburg, hiker, all 250 pounds of him, plus a knapsack that weighed almost as much, give or take a frying pan. The strongest hat in the world would have come off second-best in such an encounter. The fruit hat was annihilated.

Dora and Jane extricated the pieces from underneath Hermann (who found it difficult to stand up when he had once sat down, with the weight of his hiking equipment). They put all the pieces back into the hatbox and bore it in mournful procession back to 3 Mole Street where they emptied it out on Jane's bed.

"I expect we'll be able to mend it good as new," said Dora, hopefully.

But Jane didn't think so.

"We can call ourselves a hat hospital," said Dora, pushing her hand up inside the flattened crown of the hat in an effort to straighten it out.

They tried everything they possibly could, sewing, gluing, and even tying the broken bits of straw together, but it was no use. The hat was an absolute write-off.

"I shall have to go home now," said Dora. "What shall I say? They all know I went to get the present today."

"Tell them it's going to be a big surprise on the day," Jane suggested.

"It'll be a surprise all right," said Dora, glumly poking her finger into the collapsed pineapple. William and the twins would have some harsh words to say about a big sister who wasted all their hard-earned money, and there wasn't a penny left or anything to show for it.

"I don't mean that," said Jane. "You tell them you've left the present in my house so that your mother won't see it. I'm sure we'll think of something. When is your mother's birthday?"

"Sunday," said Dora glumly, "the day after tomorrow."

"I shall come up with something, I'm sure," said Jane.

"All right," said Dora, and she went off up the hill thinking, "And I just hope Jane does think of something, too!"

Jane had much more interesting things to think about than the present problem. When she was alone she took a little packet from her pocket and opened it.

It contained the book she had bought in the marketplace in Kilport.

THE BRACELETS
or
HABITS OF GENTLENESS
by
Miss Edgeworth

It looked exactly like the book which had appeared in her room on her very first night in Rathard; but that was not all. Inside the front cover, written in beautiful copperplate handwriting and green ink, was the following inscription:

*Know that my sweet Mary
is the owner of this book.
It anyone should steal it
'twas from Mary it was took.*

Mary.

Mary.

M.

"I think I was meant to buy it," Jane said.

CHAPTER ELEVEN

T WAS A COLD clear evening. The tide swept in around Rathard Bay and set the boats in the harbor bobbing. Cotton-wool clouds drifted over the treetops as Jane made her way up the road toward the rugged wall that surrounded the grounds of Rathard House.

The more she thought about it, the more she was convinced that the ruin held the answer to the problem of the ghost girl and, once she had decided that, something inside her kept nagging and nagging away, saying that she ought to go there.

So she went.

She passed the ruined gate-lodge, its windows sealed with corrugated tin, its garden thick with weeds, and turned up the driveway, which was choked with undergrowth. It was cold, and she hurried along, for it was already half past eight, and the night was growing on. Of course she should have waited for the morning, she knew that, but the nagging something inside her said she ought to go at once, and she could not resist the temptation.

Her feet made no sound on the carpet of pine needles and moss, but there was sound enough around her. Things rustled in the undergrowth, small birds and animals; tree branches creaked, and insects chattered busily, unaware of her intrusion.

"I am not at all afraid," she said, and her words echoed around her; and came back to make her jump.

At last the ruined walls of Rathard House loomed up out of the trees. At first she could make out only the empty windows and the chimney pots but then, as she came out of the trees onto the foot of the slope which had once been the lawn, she could see it all, the bare white bones of the conservatory and the dingy brown of the rusty metal doors which had been put up to keep out the inquisitive.

She wanted to know if the bookroom was a room in Rathard House, or if it was her own room in 3 Mole Street as it had been years ago before the Hildreths ever came there. She wanted to know so many other things about the girl in the blue velvet dress. . . . Mary, Mary. It was a nice name; she liked it.

The truth was that Jane didn't really know why she'd come, or what she expected to find. She couldn't get into the ruin, and walking 'round and 'round it wasn't likely to do much good, but something told her she *ought* to be there, and there she was.

Jane walked through the cloister arches and past the entrance to the lavender garden, making her way toward the river. If Mary had lived in Rathard House, she must often have stood by the river, watching the water cascade over the rocks and into the deep pool beneath the bridge. The day's storm had set the water in full spate, so that it roared and crashed and sprayed the overhanging branches of the trees, and foamed around the rock pools. Tall trees towered over the bridge, almost blotting out the sky and the red glow of the setting sun. White rocks shone among the gray, and moss ran down the crumbling riverbanks.

She shivered.

It was one thing to face up to the idea of a ghost in a nice warm bedroom and a friendly house, quite another to come out in the evening to a ruined house and walk around waiting for something to happen, when you had no idea what sort of something it might be.

The setting sun had caught on the top branches of a fir tree like a kite held on a slack string. It hung there lopsidedly as a cloud crept over it, sending a shadow rippling out over the ground below, across the bridge.

"I am *not* frightened," she said, through clenched teeth. Then she said it loudly, just to make sure there was no mistake about it. "I am absolutely not frightened in the very least."

Mary was too nice a person to frighten anybody.

"It is the cold that makes me shiver," she said loudly, and the crashing water seemed to catch the word "shiver" and send it racing down the river, to bounce back from the crumbling walls of Rathard House. The wind stirred and ruffled the trees and the idling cloud slid by, so that the last burning rays of the sun picked out her face again and set her shadow back behind her, the next-best thing to a companion.

She made her way to the lavender garden and pushed open the rusty gate. The high walls seemed to hold in the sweet smell of lavender, so that it was almost overpowering. Had it been Mary's own special place? There was a friendly

feel about it, despite the empty window frames
and creaking gate. Briers had laced their way up
the trellis on the red brick wall, nettles choked
the rock garden, the fountain basin was dry, and
the white lions by the path had a crust of green
slime on their smooth stone backs.

"If I stand very still," Jane thought, "and I
half close my eyes, perhaps I will be able to feel
what it used to be like." She closed her eyes and
stood very still, expecting she didn't know
what to happen, and nothing did.

She felt a bit silly.

All the way up from 3 Mole Street . . . for
what?

Jane picked some lavender and walked
around the fountain. She thought about sitting
on one of the lions, but thought better of it
when she saw the slime. Out through the arch-
way, closing the gate behind her.

The tall woman turned toward her. She
was white-haired, and she held herself stiffly,
and walked with a stick. She seemed surprised

and taken aback at seeing Jane. She put one hand to her neck, clutching at the dark-green shawl she wore.

She said one word, and one word only.

"Mary."

Jane took to her heels and fled.

A ghost is a ghost is a ghost, but you can have too much of a good thing, and Jane had just reached the end of her tether. She didn't stop running until she was halfway down the High Street in Rathard. This time she had to admit that she was well and truly frightened, but intrigued at the same time.

She had been right about Rathard House. And yet . . . if Mary had lived there . . . why did she appear in 3 Mole Street? Why didn't she haunt her own house?

That night she found herself in the book-room again but, search as she would, she could not find the original copy of *The Bracelets* to compare it with the one she had bought in Kilport. She did find *Sara Crewe* by Frances

Hodgson Burnett, and read it straight through, before she fell asleep.

She had, of course, forgotten all about the hat.

CHAPTER TWELVE

HE NEXT MORNING a telegram came for Jane.

CROSSING ON SEAGULL TONIGHT STOP
LOVE STOP MUMMY AND DADDY

It was great news! Jane was polite enough not to jump about the room and shout about it, but she couldn't altogether help her face, which broke into an allover grin and stayed that way for quite some time.

Mrs. Hildreth said, "I suppose it can't be helped," in a funny voice, which surprised Jane, who thought that she'd been a bit of a nuisance.

"It won't be dangerous, will it?" she said, suddenly anxious about Wreck Lights and lifeboats and all the other things that suggested disaster at sea. "The weather has been so changeable recently, and The Seagull is very small."

"Dangerous," said Albert, "not a bit of it." But he didn't say all he really thought. Holiday sailors weren't his cup of tea.

Jane was too pleased about her parents coming back so soon to worry about storms and shipwrecks for long.

"I suppose you'll be going home then?" said Dora, when she heard the news.

"Yes, I will," said Jane.

"Well, that's very nice of you, I must say," said Dora, sounding quite cross.

"I thought you'd be glad," said Jane. "Glad for me at any rate."

"And what about my mother's birthday hat?" said Dora.

They fell silent. Jane didn't feel that she was really responsible for the hat, because it was such a foolish choice of birthday present, and she had only put it on to please Dora, but she couldn't get away from the fact that she had put it on the spare seat and allowed a hiker to sit on it. And she had said she would do what she could to help—but how?

They went down to Gurney's Amusements and watched the man emptying the slot machines. He had a small key that opened them and he ladled out piles of grimy pennies into an apronlike bag which hung around his middle.

"If I had all that money I could buy something gorgeous," Dora said.

"But you know that no one ever wins money in arcades," Jane said. "If they did, that man's bag would have no money in it."

"I have a system," said Dora.

"Huh!"

"I have," Dora insisted. "I did it last year and I won eighteen pence. Trouble is," she added, "you need money to start with."

"I have some money," Jane said doubtfully.

"How much?" said Dora, brightening up.

"Twenty-four pence," said Jane. It was all she had left of her holiday money, but then her holiday at Rathard was almost over.

"I'm not going to let you have it to lose on those silly machines," Jane said.

"Twenty-four pence isn't enough for a present," said Dora.

"Well . . ." said Jane.

"You see that 'Goldmine' machine?" Dora said. "The one with the row of columns with silver balls in them? You fill up a column right to the top and the next ball goes into a little hole and then you get a penny for each ball in the columns below. Well, that's my system. I win on that."

"Oh, yes," said Jane, "I've seen those before. But if you count the ball that goes into the hole as well as the ones that go into the column you'll find that you get one penny less. So it takes five pennies to win four. That's not what I call sensible."

"I don't fill up the columns," said Dora. "I let other people fill them for me!"

"But you'd have to wait around for ages!" Jane said.

And they did.

At eleven o'clock Dora was three pence up, and Jane went for a walk around the harbor. When she came back Dora was two pence down.

At a quarter past twelve Dora had lost nine pence.

"I think you should stop," said Jane.

"I'll win, you wait," said Dora.

Jane went for another walk, but she didn't stay long this time, for the sky was overcast and cloudy, and it looked like rain. When she got back she met Dora at the door.

"How much have you won?" said Jane.

Silence.

"You have won something, I suppose?" Jane said, rather unkindly.

"Not exactly won," said Dora. "I would

have won if it hadn't been for that rotten machine."

"Lost?"

"Not all of it."

"How much?"

"I have ten pence left," said Dora. "It was that rotten machine. It wasn't my fault. I should have won. I played awfully cleverly and I always win."

They both went home to lunch, with an agreement to meet afterward to hold a council of war.

"It's the thought that counts," said Jane, not very convincingly. They were sitting on the sea-wall, trying to think of a present they could get for ten pence that would look like fifty-three pence worth. "I'm sure that your mother won't mind if she only gets a *little* something."

"But what am I to tell the others?" Dora said, sorrowfully.

She had a point. A "little" something would

not go down well with William Smollet or, for that matter, Barney and Sam. They had contributed a fair portion of their finances to the Birthday Fund, and they would naturally expect results.

"There must be something we could get," said Dora. She was carrying a paper bag filled with bits of the hat, and periodically she took them out and looked at them, hopefully.

"We can't get much with ten pence," said Jane.

It was so true that it would have been better left unsaid.

They went off to the harbor to look at the boats. The tide was beginning to swell a little and the sea looked angry.

"Have you read Arthur Ransome?" said Jane. "He's about boats, mostly."

"What about *Treasure Island*?" said Dora, who wanted to show Jane that she wasn't the only person in the world who had ever read a book. Jane was inclined to be a bit of a show-off about her reading, and Dora didn't like it. The Smollets had very little money and could only afford a few books of their own, although Mrs. Smollet got as many as she could for Kathleen and Dora, who were the two readers in the family. Then there was a library at school, and the once-a-fortnight bookmobile, but Dora couldn't really compete with Jane, and she knew it.

"I should say that *Treasure Island* was about treasure," Jane replied, in a rather superior-sounding voice. She stuck her nose in the air as if to show the other people on the harbor what a great deal she knew about these things. "Not *really* about boats at all," she said, sniffing.

Sticking your nose high in the air and sniffing is never a very clever thing to do, but it is exceptionally silly when you are walking along a harbor pier.

"Jane!" Dora cried, but she was too late.

All good piers come to an end somewhere,

and the one at Rathard was no exception. It came to an end and Jane walked snootily right off it.

If the tide had not been in, Jane would have come a nasty cropper. As it was she hit the water a terrible slap and swallowed a great deal of it before she came spluttering to the surface amid engine oil and seaweed.

It was a very bedraggled and disgruntled book expert who swam across to the harbor steps and made her way back up them to the anxious Dora.

"You are wet," said Dora, "and rather oily."

"Indeed you are," said the yellow-suited figure who swooped upon Jane and grabbed her. "I insist on taking you home at once, child," cried Mrs. Carew, the demon driver.

And she frog-marched Jane down the pier toward her famous motor car, the one with the racing number and the huge shiny exhaust, chattering all the way about people who went falling off piers. "Got to obey the Rules of the

Road, child," she said, "might have killed yourself if you'd fallen onto a boat."

"But I don't want to go home," said Jane desperately. She had a very sound idea of the sort of
thing Mrs. Hildreth might say if she turned up for
a second time soaked to the skin, with a fair coat-
ing of oil and seaweed smeared in her hair. Once
she might have got away with it, but twice. . . .

"Why not?" snapped Mrs. Carew.

"Because . . . because I want to help my
friend," said Jane, grasping at the first thing
that came into her mind. "My friend has a terrible problem."

"In you get," said Mrs. Carew, holding open
the car door, and pushing Jane inside. "Mind
you don't dirty my crash helmet."

"But I don't want to go!"

"Both of you," said the yellow lady, catching hold of Dora, who had been lagging behind.

"Please," said Jane, "I'll get into trouble."

Mrs. Carew climbed into the car. "One of
you will get into trouble and the other is

already in it," she said, starting the car with a roar. "That will never do. I can't have you running around like that, child," and she sent the car spinning round and shot off down the road, "so I dare say I shall have to take you to my house, and then perhaps we can sort the other trouble out as well."

"Well . . ." Jane said.

The car whizzed around the foot of Manor Street, almost knocking over a fat man with a dog. "What's your problem?" said Mrs. Carew, driving with one hand and lighting her cigar with the other. Dora told her, as she made impatient noises and changed up into top gear, where she stayed for the rest of the journey. "Doesn't sound much like trouble to me," she said. "But we'll dry out your friend and have a think about it, shall we?"

Mrs. Carew's house, when they got there, was the very reverse of her car. It was an old white cottage with a tin roof, and a rather knocked-about look to it. She lived there with her sister, Miss Agnew. "My elder sister," said Mrs. Carew, as if it mattered. She was very careful about her appearance. "You wouldn't know I was seventy, would you?" she said, biting on her cigar and swerving the car around a chicken to pull to an abrupt stop in front of the door. "There," she said. "That was a good run, wasn't it?"

"No," said the two children, who had never been driven so fast in all their lives, and didn't quite know what to make of a yellow-skirted demon driver who was old enough to be their grandmother.

"Well, I thought it was," she said, not a bit put out. "Right, the wet one goes up to the bathroom and gets out of those things. The dry one comes 'round to the back."

Jane took her things off in the bathroom and did what she could to rid herself of the tar and oil.

"I've put some clothes for you in my sister's room across the corridor," said Mrs. Carew, through the door. "I dare say they'll fit you well enough for the moment. We'll put your things by the fire. Then you'll be down for some tea. I've sent your friend off about her business, but she'll be back."

Jane was dying to know what had happened to Dora, but she didn't get a chance to ask, for she heard Mrs. Carew clatter off downstairs almost at once. She wrapped herself in a towel and nipped across the passage to Miss Agnew's room, where she found a funny long skirt and a green jersey laid out for her. They looked very old-fashioned and Jane decided that Miss Agnew must be old, for it was very much an old person's room, filled with knickknacks and dust, and not at all the sort of room that the yellow demon driver would have lived in.

She had finished putting the old clothes on—though they fitted very badly—and combing her hair, when she turned to go out of the door and, in turning, caught sight of the picture that hung over the chest of drawers.

It was a picture of a girl, a delicate water-color. She was seated at a desk, with a smiling face turned up toward the artist. In her hands she held a book, closed over, with one of her fingers carefully keeping her place, as though she'd been interrupted in the middle of an interesting bit. She had black curly hair and she wore a blue velvet dress and a dark satin shawl.

"Oh," said Jane.

She stood quite still. It was. It *was*. It just *had* to be.

"Mary," she said. "It's Mary."

"Mary Quinton," said a voice behind her, and Jane whirled 'round with her heart in her mouth, not knowing what to expect. Mrs. Carew stood in the doorway, smiling in a puzzled way. "How did you know that, child?" she said.

"I . . . I must have heard her name somewhere," Jane said. "Quinton, did you say? Do you . . . do you . . . *did* you . . ." She had so many questions she wanted to ask all at once that she couldn't think of anything to ask.

"Mary Quinton was a very dear friend of my sister's, when they were children."

Jane turned back to the picture. The pale, pretty face of the girl seemed to smile at her. "Mary Quinton," she said. It was *her* Mary. "She died, didn't she?" Jane said.

"When she was thirteen," Mrs. Carew said. "It was terribly sad. Such a happy little girl before . . . but if you really want to know more about Mary, ask my sister. I was very little at the time."

"Oh, could I, please?" Jane said eagerly.

"If you want to," said Mrs. Carew, and she took Jane downstairs and through the front room to a dark kitchen with a roaring fire where an old woman sat in a high-backed chair.

"This little girl wants to talk to you, Nell," said Mrs. Carew, drawing Jane forward.

The old woman wore a dark-green shawl, and in her hand she carried a heavy walking stick. When she saw Jane she stiffened, and for a moment they gazed at each other in amazement. It was Miss Agnew who was first to speak.

"So you *are* real," she said.

"I . . . I . . ." Jane stuttered, not sure whether or not to be frightened.

"You gave me a fright last night," Miss Agnew said. "I saw you at the house, holding lavender in your hand, and I thought that you were someone else I used to know, someone I was very fond of, once."

"Mary," said Jane. "You thought that I was Mary Quinton, didn't you? *You* thought I was a ghost!"

CHAPTER THIRTEEN

T WAS SIX o'clock before Jane
got back to 3 Mole Street.
Her clothes were dry, although they did look
and smell rather peculiar, and she had a great
deal to think about. She slipped in quietly and
changed into her best dress; then she went
downstairs and settled in the corner as though
she hadn't a care in the world.

She was annoyed with Dora. Mrs. Carew
had come up with a solution to the hat problem,
but Dora was determined to be secretive about
it.

"It is gorgeous," she said proudly, as they
made their way home.

"But what is it?"

"Wait and see," said Dora. Then she added, "I did it all myself."

And that was all she would say on the subject except to let slip that the ten pence had been spent in Mr. Russell's stationery shop in Manor Street.

"I don't believe that you could buy much for ten pence," said Jane scornfully.

"I only bought part of it," Dora said. "Mrs. Carew gave me part, and the rest I had to find for myself while you and the old woman were talking in the kitchen. What were you talking about, anyway?"

"Oh, nothing," said Jane casually. *Two* could play at secrets.

"What sort of nothing?"

"She was telling me a story," said Jane. They walked on down the street. "Aren't you going to ask me what about?" Jane said impatiently.

"No," said Dora, who was much more interested in her ten-pence mystery present, which was wrapped up in special present paper. The rain had not yet begun to fall, but the wind was rising and the sky looked dark and ominous. "I think we're in for a rough night," Mrs. Carew had said. "And they call this summer! Wouldn't you like me to run you home in the car?" But one drive in the car had been enough for both of them.

"No, thank you very much," they had said, in chorus. So they had to walk home.

"The story was about Rathard, actually," Jane said. "Miss Agnew was telling me about a little girl who used to live here."

"Somebody I know?" said Dora.

"Oh, this was long ago," Jane said. "She was called Mary Quinton and she lived up in Rathard House. Her mother was dead, you see, and she had only her father to look after her. He used to own the quarry, but things got worse and worse, and then they had to sell Rathard House and they came to live . . . guess where?"

"I don't know," said Dora, who wasn't interested.

"In the Hildreths' house, that's where," said

Jane. "And then there was the wreck, the rock-boat one, and her father was drowned. And after that Mary was very sad because she wanted her father to come back and he never would and in the end she died too, and it was all terribly terribly sad."

"Sounds silly to me," said Dora.

"She wasn't silly," Jane said hotly. "Miss Agnew knew her and used to play with her and they did such nice things together, going 'round the woods just like us, and picking lavender in the garden. And then, after the wreck, Mary just sat at home and read her books in 3 Mole Street and wouldn't come out at all and she got sick and then she died, and I don't think you ought to say she was silly. She was just lonely without her mother and father, that's all."

"All right, all right, it's only a story, isn't it? No need to get so annoyed."

Jane started to tell her that it wasn't only a story, but then she stopped.

Dora couldn't be expected to understand, so it was no use trying to explain to her. She knew that Mary Quinton wasn't silly . . . she knew because, in an odd way, she felt she knew Mary Quinton. How lonely it must have been to sit in the little room in Mole Street which had been her father's study, surrounded by books, knowing that he would never come back. How terrible it must have been for Mary when the ship went down off Hammer Island, and she knew that he had gone down with it.

Jane was quiet at tea, so much so that Mrs. Hildreth thought that something must be the matter with her.

"Are you tired, dear?" she said.

"Just thinking," said Jane.

"What about?"

"What it would be like to be alone," she said. "Suppose I had no father and mother—wouldn't that be awful?"

"But you have, dear, haven't you?"

"But supposing I hadn't," Jane insisted. "It

would be awfully lonely for me, wouldn't it? I'd only have my books, and I'd just sit and read all day and I . . . I . . ."

"But you'd have all your friends, wouldn't you?" said Mrs. Hildreth, interrupting her. "You really mustn't get upset about things that are not going to happen, Jane."

Jane wanted to say, "But it has happened. It happened to Mary, and I know how it felt!" But she knew she couldn't. Nobody would understand her. But she *did* know.

"I just have a funny feeling, that's all," she said, and she would say no more.

The wind roared among the chimney tops, and in the back room of 3 Mole Street they could hear the sea breaking on the seawall, and the incessant pitter-patter of the rain on the kitchen roof. They piled the fire high and clustered 'round it. Albert, Jane, Mrs. Hildreth, and . . . and . . .

"They wouldn't try to cross tonight, would they?" Jane said suddenly.

Albert Hildreth looked grave. "I hope not," he said. "I'm sure they wouldn't. Not on a night like that. Not unless . . ."

"Unless what?"

"Unless they started early, before the storm blew up," he said. Then he saw the look on Jane's face. "But I'm sure they wouldn't."

Jane said nothing. She sat looking at the fire. Then she raised her head and looked at Mary.

Mary smiled back at her.

Jane went to bed early.

The roar of the lifeboat gun wakened her. It boomed, and boomed again, shaking the house.

She sat up in bed.

"Oh, no," she said, "oh, no."

Boom.

She heard Albert shouting something, and then he went down the stairs three at a time, and the front door slammed. She could hear his running feet in the street outside, joined by others.

Quickly, Jane got out of bed and rushed to the window. A crowd was already gathering on the pier and, as she watched, a flare erupted from the sea, just to the east of the Wreck Light, and broke into a thousand stars.

Mrs. Hildreth came softly into the room.

"You should be in bed, dear," she said.

"It's *The Seagull*, isn't it?" Jane said. "Don't say it isn't. I know it is."

"We don't know," Mrs. Hildreth said. "It could be." She bit her lip. "I'm sure they'll be all right, really I am. You mustn't worry. Look, they're getting the boat out now. They'll be putting to sea in a minute."

Jane turned back to the window. The lifeboat looked so small, and the waves were huge and dark, lashed by the wind, bursting in spray against the boat's bows. The light of Rathard Harbor and the Wreck Light cut across each other . . . but out there on the sea, bearing down on the rocks of Hammer Island . . . what hope could *The Seagull* have?

"They'll go on the rocks," Jane said. "I know they will. Like the old rock boat."

"They can see the rocks," said Mrs. Hildreth. "There's a light there. That's what it's there for."

"But the sea?" Jane said, as the waves pounded on the shore.

"Go to bed. I'll bring you up a cup of something, and we can wait together." Mrs. Hildreth could see that Jane would not rest. She couldn't leave the window, not when her father and mother were out there in the storm, not when she could see the bobbing lights of the lifeboat as it fought its way out to them.

Mrs. Hildreth took a blanket and wrapped it around Jane, then she slipped out of the room and went downstairs. She knew that it would be a long night for both of them, and she was frightened, too—frightened for Jane, and frightened for Albert.

"But they have the Wreck Light now," she

said. "They won't go on the rocks; they can see them."

The wind rattled the windowpanes and Jane shivered. She could almost imagine what it would be like out there as the little *Seagull* battled to and fro amid the waves, trying desperately to clear the point of Hammer Island.

"Please please please let them be all right," she said out loud. She closed her eyes and prayed it. She prayed so long that she quite lost track of time. Then she opened her eyes again, and looked out of the window.

It had grown very dark.

She could see little lights moving on the pier, and hear voices calling but . . . there was something odd about it all, something disjointed. What had happened to the streetlights? There were no lampposts.

There was no Wreck Light!

She twitched back heavy red drapes and peered anxiously out. What had happened? Why was the place the same, yet different?

Red drapes . . .

Then she knew what had happened and why there was no Wreck Light.

She drew back from the window, half afraid, and looked around her as the soft glow of the gas jet played over the books, gleaming brown and red and purple in the shadows. The green library steps sat against the wall, and the funny carved pipes which had once belonged to Henry Quinton lay disused in their rack.

The wind roared again and the gaslight flickered, reminding her of her own father and mother, and the terrible thing which was happening to them.

"Oh, please," she said, out loud.

Jane turned back to the window.

Mary Quinton took her hand. The sleeve of the blue velvet dress was trimmed in white lace, and her brown eyes were puckered in concern. She drew Jane toward the window where they both stood, staring out at the night and the dark stormy sea.

"It will be all right, won't it?" Jane said.

The hand that held hers was warm to the touch, and she felt a great sense of warmth and comfort creep over her.

"It will be all right, Mary, won't it?"

When Mrs. Hildreth came back to the room she found, to her surprise, that Jane had fallen asleep at the window. The flash of the Wreck Light cut across the sea, and the storm still raged, but Jane knew nothing about it.

"Poor thing," Mrs. Hildreth said.

She picked Jane up and carried her back to bed where she tucked the clothes around her little guest. Jane stirred in her sleep, but she did not wake, and Mrs. Hildreth went away as quietly as she could, taking the laden tray with her.

It was strange, she thought, how contentedly the child slept, when she had been so concerned only a matter of minutes before.

* * *

"Wake up! Wake up!"

Someone was shaking Jane.

She opened her eyes and . . .

"Daddy!"

Her father's face smiled down at her. He was tired and pale-looking and all wrapped up in a funny sort of yellow raincoat, but he was safe, safe and sound. And there was her mother, too, coming into the room behind him, all wrapped up in a blanket. Outside she could hear people talking and laughing, and Albert's cheery voice rocking the rafters.

Jane was out of bed in a second, and she flew straight into her mother's arms. She waltzed around the room in excitement, chattering away.

Then, quite suddenly, she stopped.

"Why, what is it, child?" said Mrs. Hildreth. "You look as though you'd seen a ghost."

"Oh, nothing," said Jane.

She was looking at Mary. The little ghost

stood beside Jane's father, with her arm almost touching his. She looked, Jane thought, just a little wistful, but suddenly she clapped her hands as she had at the party, and her face broke into a most unghostlike grin. Then she pulled her satin shawl around her shoulders and . . .

. . . and Jane lost sight of her, as her Uncle Tom came barging into the room. One minute Mary was there, and the next she was gone.

Jane never saw her again.

CHAPTER FOURTEEN

SN'T IT," SAID Dora, "positively the most gorgeous thing you have ever seen, not counting the hat?"

"It is very nice," said Jane, and for once she meant it. The picture was very nice, and a particularly Smollety present. Dora had made it with shells and leaves and seaweed and driftwood glued onto stiff cardboard and painted. She had put all these things together to make up a picture of a house with ten people walking around it—one of whom, unmistakably, wore a hat.

"That's us!" said Dora proudly. After all, she had made it all herself for only two shillings, the cost of the glue and the cardboard from Mr. Russell's. Everything else in the picture she had had to look for on Mrs. Carew's instructions and she really had made a good job of it—if there was a piece of punctured plastic pineapple in it, so much the better!

Mrs. Smollet thought that it was beautiful, and said so.

Three of the small Smollets and Tobias thought that it was splendid.

William Smollet thought that it was soppy. But then, as Jane pointed out to him, he hadn't seen the fruit hat, and goodness knows what he would have made of that.

The Saved-from-the-Sea party for the Reids somehow got mixed up in Mrs. Smollet's birthday celebrations and turned that particular Sunday into a long party, with a great deal of coming and going and congratulating afoot. Yet Jane was conscious through all the fun of someone who wasn't there.

Toward evening, she slipped quietly out and made her way to the ruins of Rathard House.

It was about an hour later when they started looking for her, because the Reids wanted to start back to Belfast.

But they couldn't find her, which wasn't really surprising, for no one thought of looking in the graveyard.

Jane had cleared away the weeds from the small lopsided stone and placed a sprig of lavender before it. Then she stood back, wanting to say something, but not quite knowing what.

"It didn't happen this time, did it?" she said.

And then, "You didn't want my help at all, did you? You were helping me. I got it all wrong."

But if Jane hoped to see Mary Quinton just once more, she was disappointed. She never told anyone what had happened, for she didn't think that they would believe her. It was her secret. The nearest she got to saying anything about it was when they asked where she had been.

"I was saying good-bye to a friend."